Celia Rees writes: I am interested in the way that the past underlies the present; how perfectly ordinary places, otherwise hardly worth a second glance, are shadowed by sinister events from the past. Many of our ancient cities host ghost walks which invite us to visit such places and it was on just such a walk that I had the idea for this series. I found myself thinking: What if there were two cities? The one we live in – and one that ghosts inhabit. What if at certain times of the year and in certain places, the barriers between the two worlds grow thin, making it possible to move from one to the other? And if ghosts lived there, why not others? Creatures we know from myth and legend, creatures so powerful that even the ghosts fear them? Just a story? Maybe. But on a recent visit to that city, I found that several of the ghost walk routes had been abandoned, because of poltergeist activity . . .

Celia Rees has written many books for children and teenagers and enjoys writing in different genres. She hopes what interests her will interest other people, be it ghosts, vampires, UFOs or witch trials. Her latest books, *Truth or Dare* and *Witch Child*, have been published to critical acclaim.

Other titles available from Hodder Children's Books:

City of Shadows

CELIA REES

Hodder
Children's
Books

a division of Hodder Headline Limited

For my friend, Katy,
and for Lydia

First published as separate volumes:
H is for Haunting and *A is for Apparition* in 1998
by Hodder Children's Books

This bind-up edition published in 2001
by Hodder Children's Books Limited

10 9 8 7 6 5 4

A Catalogue record for this book
is available from the British Library

ISBN 0 340 81800 X

Typeset by Hewer Text Ltd, Edinburgh
Printed and bound in Great Britain by
Clays Ltd, St Ives plc

The paper and board used in this paperback by Hodder
Children's Books are natural recyclable products made from
wood grown in sustainable forests. The manufacturing processes
conform to the environmental regulations of the country of origin.

Hodder Children's Books
A Division of Hodder Headline Limited
338 Euston Road
London NW1 3BH
www.madaboutbooks.com

Midsummer

City of Shadows

All through the city and its suburbs, the past lies behind the present and ghosts shadow the living. There are threshold zones, borderlines, and places where the laws of time and space falter. Strange things can happen, the barriers between the worlds grow thin and it is possible, just possible, to move from one world to another . . .

'What does it say again?' Kate Williams asked.

Her brother Davey reached in his pocket for the crumpled piece of paper, flattened it out on his jeans and held it up for them to see.

Haunts Tours

Horrible.Awful.Unusual.Nasty.Terrifying.Sinister. Definitely not for the nervous!

7:30pm: Market Cross

COST: £5 Adults, £4 Students, £3 Children

We are alone . . . or are we? Follow the Ghost Trail down shadowed cobbled streets, along narrow alleys and into the hidden underground vaults which lie at the secret heart of the old city. Glimpse another world, one populated by ghosts, ghouls, spirits and spectres of every kind – but beware! Keep alert at all times! Stay with your guide! You will be visiting places where past and present combine – especially when the daylight drains away . . .

'And you don't want to go?' Kate squinted down at him. 'But you've been nagging on about it for ages! I just don't understand. You can be such a pain some-times!'

'I just thought we could go to Pizza Hut. Spend the money there instead,' Davey muttered.

'But why?'

His twin cousins, Tom and Elinor, flicked back their sandy fringes and stared at him; their heads set at the same angle, the same expression on their freckled faces, the same quizzical look in their greeny-grey eyes. Davey's own dark brown eyes looked from one to the other. Sometimes they could be unnerving, like seeing in stereo.

Davey looked at the ground and mumbled something.

'What? Say what?' Tom cupped a hand behind his ear.

Davey stuffed his hands in his pockets and shook his head. It was difficult to explain. He did not want them thinking he was scared or anything. He just had a bad feeling. He'd had them before, and when he did some-thing awful nearly always happened. Gran had them, too. She had a long word for it: premonition. Davey shivered. That's what he'd just had – a premonition.

'Anyway, it's *our* birthday treat, not yours,' Tom pointed out when Davey did not say anything. 'So we get to choose.'

'Let's take a vote,' Elinor suggested. 'Save an argu-ment.'

All hands raised except his own. Davey did not want to give in, but to explain his reluctance would invite mick-taking, particularly from Tom, who had no time for superstition. It had been Davey's idea. He had been the one to see the Ghost Walk advert and say it looked cool. Tom and Ellie were staying for the weekend and had jumped at the suggestion. They had all come in from the suburbs on purpose. Even in his own mind, all those reasons outranked a mere feeling. He shrugged his shoulders and followed them. He had no way of knowing how much he would come to regret that decision.

They were moving away from the New Town's shopping centre with its fast food outlets. The new clock tower said nearly twenty past seven. Not even time to grab a burger, he thought, as they walked along Broad Street which fronted the river. He glanced across the water up to the Old Town's higgledy-piggledy stone and slate outlined against the sky. The evening was still light, midsummer-blue bright, but it already looked dark over there. The buildings stood like black, jagged teeth against strange, yellowy-grey clouds which were dull and shiny at the same time, like brass that needed to be cleaned. Looking at it gave Davey that funny feeling again. 'Goose walking over your grave', that's what Gran always said. Davey rubbed at his arms. If that was the case, a whole flock must be on top of his grave, tramping backwards and forwards.

The crowd had thickened round the traffic crossing at the bottom of New Bridge Street which led across the busy road to the river side. The people surged forward as the lights changed to walking green. Davey was just about

3

to join them, when a little kid came hurtling out of the moving mass.

'Hey, steady!'

The child charged towards him, looking over his shoulder. He would have crashed right into him if Davey had not put out a hand to slow him down. The boy was young, not more than four or five, dressed in a bright ladybird-red zip-up top. Davey looked down into the big blue-grey eyes. He had never seen anyone so terrified.

'Are you OK?'

The child shook his head.

'Have you lost your mum, your dad?' Davey asked, bending down to be on the same level as him.

The boy nodded slowly as the lights blinked back to STOP. Suddenly there was a woman standing behind him. Her hand came down, long slim red-tipped fingers took the child by the shoulder. Davey looked up into a face, pretty but very pale, framed by silver-blonde hair. The woman's red-lipsticked mouth was smiling.

'Is this your mum?' Davey asked the little boy, who shook his head violently.

'No!' The expression in his eyes deepening to purest fear.

The woman's smile widened, sharp and shark-like. Davey's own smile faltered as the slanted grey eyes narrowed and held him, the irises glinting silver, like ice on steel. The look she gave him held him frozen, the chill seeping deep, right through to his bones . . .

'Davey? Are you all right?' Kate's voice sounded muffled and far away. He looked up at her, his vision blurred, as though he was seeing through water.

'Yes. I guess.' His speech was croaky and thick as if he had been asleep. His head felt muzzy, empty, like someone had wiped his circuits.

'I thought you were right behind me. I had to come back. And I find you rooted to the spot, staring into space, like . . .' Kate broke off. 'Are you sure you're all right? You look a bit funny.'

'I'm fine.' Davey tried to put on a reassuring smile. 'There was something . . .' He looked round, suddenly remembering the woman and the little boy. 'Did you see them?'

'See who?'

'A woman and a little boy. They were standing right there . . .'

'I didn't see anyone – just you in a dream. Quick – the lights are changing!'

Kate grabbed his hand and pulled him across the road. As soon as they reached the central reservation, Davey looked back, scanning the pavement opposite, but he could not see the woman or the child. The lights changed again and he followed Kate over the other half of the road towards the long concrete bridge that separated the new from the old part of the city. Wide gardens stretched either side of the broad river. All through the summer there were open-air cafés, Punch and Judy shows, clowns

5

and jugglers; perhaps the woman had taken the little boy down there? Davey leaned over the railing, watching the people, but still he could see no sign of them.

'Come on, Davey. What *is* the matter with you?'

Kate had hold of his arm again and was dragging him along the pavement by his coat sleeve. Davey was about to protest; he hated it when she did this: behaved like she was Mum and he was a tiresome little kid. He was just going to pull away from her when he stopped. Davey looked at the people around them, wandering tourists, strolling families, and had that odd feeling: as if this had happened before, or was waiting to happen. It gave him a strange queasy feeling deep down inside.

'This ghost walk thing was your idea . . .' Kate was saying, her voice coming and going like a poorly-tuned radio. 'If you don't hurry we'll miss the start . . . it won't be worth going . . . Tom and El are waiting . . .'

Kate joined their cousins and together they walked over the new bridge. Davey followed them up towards the Cannongate whose massive stone archway stood like a mouth at the entrance to the Old Town. It was at the side of the road, traffic diverted around it, one of the four gates which allowed access to the least changed and most haunted part of the ancient city. The others went through laughing and joking, but something made Davey hesitate. He did not want to enter the dank, chill space. He looked up at the squat stone tower with strange feelings of fear, of foreboding, sweeping over him. Part of him was hoping that the Ghost Walk had started without them; that they would be too late, that they would not have to go on it. A shiver went down his spine. The geese were on his grave again – big time.

2

They walked up Bridge Street and rounded the great stone bulk of the cathedral with its smartly painted black and gold railings. Quite a few people were already assembled on the other side of the square, standing on the cobblestones under the stunted remains of the old market cross. A group of American tourists and some Japanese students, probably studying English at one of the City colleges, were gathered at the board marked H.A.U.N.T.S. A German couple were translating the notice board, reading it out to each other.

ONLY PAY AN OFFICIAL GUIDE, the notice said. YOUR OFFICIAL GUIDE TONIGHT IS: *Louise* had been chalked into the space provided. Louise, a dark-haired, chubby girl in a long black dress, was collecting in money and giving out tickets. Her staff of thick twisted wood with a plastic skull on the top lay propped against the base of the market cross next to her cloak and bag. Louise was made up to look scary and dramatic. Purple lipstick matched her nail varnish and her eyes were heavily shadowed, outlined in black.

'No unaccompanied children under twelve,' she said, eyeing them doubtfully when they got to the front of the queue.

'I'm thirteen,' Kate said. Tall, with her long fair hair tied back, she could have passed for even older.

'We're twelve,' the twins chipped in. 'We've just had a birthday.'

'What about him?'

His twelfth birthday was only a couple of months away, but Davey was small for his age, though sturdily built. He tensed despite himself and he could feel the blood beating up into his face as the guide scowled in his direction.

'He's twelve, too,' Kate said quickly.

'He looks kind of small to me . . .'

'So?' Kate shrugged. 'He'll grow. Here.' She pulled money out of her pocket. 'Four at three pounds each. Twelve pounds exactly, I think.' She handed over the notes and coins and held out her hand.

'OK. OK,' the girl sighed as she ripped tickets out of her book, 'but do as I say. Stay close to me and don't go wandering away. Especially not in the vaults. I can't be held responsible . . .'

'Of course,' Kate cut in, eyebrows rising as if to say: we aren't stupid, what do you take us for?

When everyone assembled had bought tickets, and she'd decided no one else would turn up, Louise picked up her staff, clipped on her cloak and started. She had clearly done this lots of times before, but several people stepped back startled. The girl was transformed. Her grumpiness disappeared as she paced up and down beneath the ancient market cross. A couple of the Americans jumped as she began yelling in a loud voice, waving her arms about and pointing.

'Did you know,' she began, 'that in this very square, the very place where we are standing now, vast crowds would regularly gather to see murderers *hanged*, witches *burnt* and traitors *drawn and quartered*? Do you know what that means?' She scanned her own small gathering with narrowed eyes. Several people nodded, but Davey knew she was going to tell them anyway. 'Hearts *torn* still beating from the traitor's chest, intestines *ripped out* and wound round a stick . . .'

She was shouting now, her voice booming and echoing back from the front of the cathedral and the other buildings in the square. Her dramatic display was attracting attention from members of the public who had not paid for the Haunts Tour. Davey stepped back, partly out of embarrassment and partly to avoid the long necklaces she wore: rosary beads and five pointed stars flying dangerously about.

'We move on from this place of public execution to walk the blood-drenched ghost-haunted streets and learn the secret history of this ancient city. From there we will visit the underground vaults of the *hidden city*, the part that people *never* see. You will hear stories of plague, starvation, death and destruction; meet with horrible spectres, some fearful, some pitiful . . .'

She continued to talk as she led them off at a brisk pace, to the top of the Market Square.

'This road is a continuation of Bridge Street and contains the law courts and some of the city's grandest buildings. It is called Fore Street because it was the foremost thoroughfare leading up from Cannongate.' She recited from memory. 'It is called Cannongate because, years ago, a cannon would go off at sunset to warn the population that curfew was falling.'

Nothing very dramatic about that, so Louise added a very loud BOOM making the American women jump again. Louise smiled a little in satisfaction. They hadn't even got to the scary part yet.

'Now,' she said, skirts swirling. 'If you will follow me. Down here . . .'

She changed direction so abruptly that several of her party almost fell over each other as they left the square and the main thoroughfare with its impressive banks and law courts. They were in the legal and civic centre of the city. Busy enough by day, the whole district was more or less deserted after the offices closed.

They turned sharp right into a cobbled passageway with narrow, cracked pavements. Tall grey buildings rose high on either side giving out a chill and cutting off what was left of the light. People shivered and one American lady pulled her cardigan tighter round herself, even before Louise had begun to describe whatever bloodcurdling events had happened here.

'This is Fetter Lane,' Louise was saying. 'The name is really from the old French for lawyer, but local people believe it refers to the prisoners fettered in the jail at the side of the court house. Here we can see one of the original entrances . . .' They crowded round the squat, grey wooden door, studded with iron, and as they peered through the rusting bars the shiver became more general. 'It is said that, on certain nights, the howling of the inmates can be heard, and the dark figure of the notorious highwayman Jack Cade can be seen pacing to and fro, his chains rattling and dragging across the floor . . .'

Her last remark was accompanied by the clanking chink of iron links. Louise had taken a length of chain from her bag and was pulling it along the ground. She allowed herself a slight smirk as some of the group let out gasps and leapt into the air, while the others looked around frightened and startled.

'What a cheesy trick!' Davey commented when he realised what the guide had done.

'She got you going, though.' Kate grinned. 'I thought you were going into orbit!'

'She scared me, too.' Elinor smiled at Davey.

'Not me.' Tom shook his head. 'I saw it a mile off. Ahh, what's that?'

He jumped away as his sister walked her fingers up his back.

'You were as scared as anyone, Tom. You are such a blagger!'

Tom turned to get his sister but the group was moving on under an arch and into another narrow passageway.

Their footsteps sounded loud on the cobbled floor of Fiddler's Court, echoing off the buildings crowded in on either side. Louise stopped in front of what had once been a grand town house. Polished brass plaques shone beside the big front door.

'As you can see,' Louise started, 'this is now mostly accountants' and solicitors' offices, but it was once the abode of Judge Andrews. He was known as the Executioner, because he sent so many to their deaths. A devout churchgoer and a godly man by day, he led a double life. Eventually he was arrested for witchcraft himself and accused of the most terrible crimes. He mounted the gallows steps in the summer of 1670. This house stood unoccupied for more than a century, an object of *horror* where *hauntings* are rumoured to occur.'

A chill little wind stole between them and several people moved closer together.

Louise nodded sympathy. 'Many people do feel the odd shiver here and some of the psychics who come on our tours have sensed and even seen dark presences that they swear to be *pure evil*. Not that way,' she added as the German couple wandered towards Blythe Lane. 'That's a dead end. This way, please.'

Davey was at the back as Louise led them briskly through Fiddler's Court and off down Quarry Street. There was no one about. There were no late-night shops here; nothing to attract the evening tourists. There were no pubs in this particular warren of streets and the tea shops and restaurants closed early. The whole area seemed deserted apart from their party. He stopped, half-thinking he heard a footfall behind him and a laugh as light as the sigh of wind in the trees; but there was no wind, and no trees either. He turned, but no one was there. He rubbed at the goosebumps on his arms. The street ran gently downhill and towards the bottom the buildings were getting older, changing to half-timber. Davey's feeling that they should not be here was coming back again and getting stronger . . .

'Hurry up, you there.' Louise was frowning at him, 'I warned you against dawdling. Now, as I was saying . . .' the group had turned left and were standing about halfway down a narrow side street called Butcher's Row. 'Before this became a Tourist Information Office, it used to be a public house, an inn called *The Seven Dials*. A most *notorious* place.' She waved her arms at the large half-timbered building. 'The abode of Jack Cade, who I mentioned earlier. He met his end hanging from a noose in Market Square. They do say . . .' Louise lowered her voice and beckoned for them to come towards her. 'They do say that on dark nights, when the moon is shining, you can still hear the beat of hooves along Harrow Lane. The clatter and clash on the cobbles as he turns into the yard to visit his sweetheart, Polly Martin, the innkeeper's daughter, who was shot by the Revenue Men as she tried to warn him of the trap that they had set for him.'

They all stared, caught in wonder at being at the actual

site of such terrible events. The black-and-white frontage stared back. It did not look particularly scary now. The windows were full of notices and Tourist Information stickers. The top part, which straddled the archway that led to the courtyard, had been made into a gallery. Next door was a café. There was a menu on the railings outside it and chairs and tables set ready for tea and coffee. Davey thought he heard that laugh again and glanced up to see a white face; but it must have been a trick of the light on the diamond panes. He blinked and it had gone.

'I've heard that before,' Tom was saying. 'It's a poem. We did it at school.'

'So?' Louise gave him a hard look. 'It's still a matter of historical record,' she added pompously. 'Look it up if you don't believe me. Now, ladies and gentlemen,' she turned to the rest of them. 'This way, if you please.'

She led them past the Tourist Information Office and off down a narrow crooked alley: Johnswell Passage.

'We are now going into the oldest part of the city. Some of the foundations here date back to Roman times. As you can see,' she stretched her arms out, nearly touching the walls on either side, 'the buildings are very close together. This led to a very unhealthy environment. In the centre of the street, we can still see the common gutter. All the waste from the houses either side, and Butcher's Row nearby, would have been deposited here.' Louise smiled as several noses wrinkled.

'This collected filth seeped into the water supply, the

Johnswell. This ancient well was sited just about here.' She paused at a spot on the corner where the alley opened out into another road. 'It was destroyed in Victorian times. One local doctor said it had been responsible for more deaths than all the wars put together. Close proximity of so many people living together also helped the spread of *plague* . . .'

She stopped on Harrow Lane to let the name of the dread disease sink in.

'This building was once a pest house.' She pointed to a craft shop with a thick wooden door. 'The plague was particularly bad in this part of the city. Victims would break out in a slight red rash – at first. But soon the spots turned to *great weeping sores*, then they developed *buboes like huge black boils* and *began coughing and spitting blood*.' Louise smiled again at the effect she was having, it was part of her job to creep them out. She began walking up and down chanting, 'Bring out your dead, bring out your dead,' in a mournful doomy voice.

Davey looked away, embarrassed again. Up ahead the street looked different, he half expected to see a cart creaking towards them.

'There was no hope, poor dears,' Louise was saying. 'The infected were brought to this house and kept in isolation, boarded up and guarded for forty days to prevent the disease from spreading. The plague led to mass panic. No one was safe. The mob would riot for days. It was the most lawless time in the city's long history.

16

Eventually they stopped boarding up individual houses and bricked up whole streets instead. Hundreds died, thousands even. Some say up to two thirds of the population. But more of that in the underground city – which is where we are going now.'

Louise turned, staff waving, cloak swirling, and set off again, leading them down the steep cobbled street towards a flight of stone steps marked Keeper's Stairs. Davey stopped for a moment to look back at the pest house, his mind still lingering on the horror it had contained. Grass seemed to sprout between the cobble stones and for a moment he thought he saw the shape of a cross, dripping what looked like blood, on the craft shop's heavy front door . . .

It might simply be the sunset splashing the street with red, but the chill down his spine was real enough. He was suddenly aware of how quiet it was, no sound from anywhere, no sound at all. The hairs stirred on his head, creeping up the back of his neck. Again he had that feeling: something odd was happening. He set off at a run and clattered down the flight of stone steps, not wanting to be left alone for another second.

3

There was a door set into the wall towards the bottom of the steps. Davey followed the tour group through it and found them crowding down a narrow underground tunnel.

'Welcome,' Louise was saying in her best scary voice. 'Welcome to the *terror*, the *mystery* that is the *hidden* city.' She paced up and down, swinging her lantern, making the shadows dance and fall across the ceiling and down the thick stone walls. 'I'd like to take you back to 1645. The city is in the grip of plague and in this area, Cairncross Close, and all the little streets around about, it is especially bad. So bad that this whole area is known as the Plague Quarter. Now,' she looked round, reading their expressions as her lamp gleamed on their faces. 'What did the authorities do? What would you do?' She flashed the light again but got no answers, just a few puzzled shrugs. 'Brick up the streets, of course! Yes! That's what the authorities did. Seal the whole lot off! Until every last person is *dead*! Nearly *two hundred people* met this terrible fate!'

Kate noted Davey's entrance, but most of her attention was on Louise. Horror crept through her as the guide described how, when the streets were opened up, bodies were dragged out, loaded into carts and taken to one of the massive plague pits outside the town. Kate shivered. It was not just the chill of the tale that made her slip her sweatshirt over her head. It was cold down here, that deep, stone cold which quickly takes away body heat and seeps into your bones.

'After the plague abated nobody would live here,' Louise went on. 'Even the poorest shunned these streets; no one would walk through, even by daylight. Houses, shops, remained empty for seventy years or more until the authorities had a bright idea. The city was becoming overcrowded again. Space was at a premium. So they simply levelled off the tops of the buildings and *built over them*. There are roads above here, and houses. Look up there.' She pointed to crystalline deposits hanging like icicles from the rough stone roof. 'You can see where the salt soaks through from the modern road surface.'

They were standing in a subterranean street. On either side gaps in the stone marked actual windows and doors.

'How many people up there,' Louise pointed again at the ceiling, 'how many people know that they are walking on a true ghost city? A realm where the dead hold sway . . .'

She led them to one of the side rooms and they all peered in.

'Some of these rooms are hired out to groups of modern witches who hold meetings here to practise *magic*! Not black magic,' she added quickly, 'nothing sinister like that. White magic. Perfectly harmless. This,' she pressed a switch and the room was bathed in eerie violet light, 'is such a room. Groups use this for their meetings. We cannot go in, I'm afraid. It is locked.' She gripped the wrought-iron gate which blocked it off. 'But you are welcome to take a look.'

Kate peered through the jostle of people in front of her. The room was painted and draped in purple and black. It smelt of stale incense and old wax. Huge candles, partly burnt down, stood on high stands. The floor was marked out with a large circle and a five-pointed star.

'Is that a mirror, over there in the corner?' one of the American women asked.

Kate looked over to where she was pointing. A large mirror in an ornate gold frame stood against the far wall. The surface was misted, diffusing the light shining on to it; the interior reflected was velvety dark and deep.

'Yes,' Louise answered quietly. She was not shouting now, or telling a story. She licked her lips and sounded almost nervous. 'Ever since it came here, there has been a problem with condensation. See?' Her lamp showed droplets of water oozing down the walls and forming on the tiny stalactites hanging from the low ceiling. 'It was bone-dry in here before. Some of the group think it's a portal, you know? Some kind of doorway to a different dimension. They want it out of here.'

A few of her audience grinned at that, they were becoming used to Louise and her efforts to scare them; but there was a difference in her face, and her voice carried a note of real fear for the first time, instead of the mock terror she was paid to mime.

'Let's move on, shall we?'

Louise led them over to the cobbler's shop opposite, her voice going back to normal as she began to describe the band of ghosts living in it.

Davey was at the back of the shuffling queue of people which made him the last to see the Room of Ceremonies. He had never seen such a strange place. He leaned over the iron gate to get a better look and felt it give way under his weight. It was not locked, despite what Louise had said. A quick look behind showed the rest of them listening to Louise, so Davey gave the gate an experimental push . . .

Guided by curiosity, Davey sneaked into the room with its weird insignias and painted signs. It was not square, as he'd thought, or round either. It was octagonal. He crossed the circle and walked round the large five-pointed star painted in the middle. If he had known about such things, he would have noticed that two points of the star were angled up, like a set of horns: the symbol of black magic, not white. But he did not.

He stepped over the chalked lines and into the centre, careful not to scuff the strange markings. In front of him was the misted mirror. It showed another mirror, set opposite. They were fixed at an angle to reflect each other. A series of dark rooms got smaller and smaller, going on forever, with him in the centre. The effect was strange. Unsettling. Davey moved nearer, compelled to look closer . . .

He went right up to it, his breath thickening the mist on the glass. He found himself leaning forward, palms against the surface, trying to look past himself, trying to see how far the reflections went. On to infinity, or so they said. Was it possible to see that far? As he peered in further, the room behind him, even his own reflection seemed to disappear. There was only the mist, but it seemed on the inside now, not the outside, swirling in long curling patterns, pulling him deeper and deeper, until he went right through the wall.

4

'And when they looked again, he wasn't there! He had *completely disappeared*!'

Louise held the lantern under her chin to make herself look even more frightening. She lowered her voice dramatically as she finished the ghost story she was telling, her eyes gleaming in shadowed sockets as she delivered the punch line.

Kate started in alarm as someone jogged her arm. She turned round, furious. Who was making her jump like that? If it was Davey, she'd kill him.

But it was not her brother, it was Elinor, trying to attract her attention.

'What?' she hissed. 'I'm listening!'

'It's Davey,' Elinor whispered back. 'He's not here.'

'What do you mean, not here?'

'What I said. He's not anywhere. Is he, Tom?'

Her brother shook his head

Kate craned her neck, trying to see past the people behind and to the side. The twins were right: no sign. Trust Davey to do something stupid. Why did he have to spoil everything? This was just so typical . . .

After a moment or two fear began to worm at her insides, eating into the anger. With it came guilt. She was the eldest. She was supposed to be responsible. Kate chewed her lip. What were they going to do?

'Er, excuse me . . .'

She pushed to the front where Louise was in full flow.

'Yes,' the guide scowled, 'what is it?'

'My brother, he's not here . . .'

The rest of the group looked round searching, as if he might be hiding by their feet, or under their coats, or something.

'Not here?' Louise repeated, using her ordinary voice this time.

'No,' Kate shook her head.

'What does he look like?'

'About so high.' Kate indicated her shoulder. 'He's got dark hair and, and he's wearing a white T-shirt and jeans. I – I thought he was just behind us, but—'

'He can't have got past me. There's only one way, as you can see.' Louise held her lantern high. The darkness swallowed the light as the tunnel stretched away. 'Perhaps he's back the way we came in.'

'Maybe he went out again,' one of the American women said. 'Maybe he's afraid of the dark and, you know, enclosed spaces.'

Kate frowned. That didn't sound like Davey. On the other hand, he *had* been behaving strangely.

'Yes,' she agreed. 'Maybe that's it. In that case,' she looked down at Elinor and Tom, 'We'd better go back and look for him.'

'If you go out,' Louise warned, 'you can't come in again. The door locks automatically. We can't have people wandering in off the street. The vaults and tunnels go on for miles and are largely unexplored. Also, I can't give a refund to anyone leaving a Haunts Tour . . .'

'That's OK.' Kate was already walking away.

'Take this,' Louise called after her. Reaching into her bag, she fished out a torch. 'Check the side chambers.'

'Thanks.' Kate took it from her, clicking the button to see that it was working.

'You can put it just inside the door as you let yourselves out.'

Just for a moment, Louise wondered if she should call the girl back. They were not supposed to let people leave, especially not in the vaults. Kids on their own were trouble. She should have known as soon as she saw them. She was a guide, not a play-group leader. She should not have let them join in the first place. On the other hand, the tour down here had only just started and they were near enough to the entrance . . .

She turned to the rest of the group. 'Now, as I was saying . . .'

The next scary story faded as Kate, Tom and Elinor went back the way they had come. They looked in each doorway, half expecting Davey to be hiding and ready to jump out at them, but there was no sign of him. Each chamber was empty.

25

'Wait a minute,' Tom said as they reached the first pair of rooms. 'Didn't she say this was locked?'

'Yes,' Kate answered, coming over to him.

'Well, it's not.'

Tom pushed. The gate barring access to the Room of Ceremonies swung open under his touch.

5

Davey looked round in surprise, not exactly sure how he got outside. There must have been another door behind the mirror, because he was out on the steps. The wall behind him was smooth, he ran his hands over it, solid stone. It offered no route back. Still, there was always the way he had gone in. He went down the steps a little way and tried the door used by Haunts Tours. It was locked. He would just have to wait for them to come out again. Davey looked about, thinking what to do. He was not sure how long they'd be, and it was already chilly down here between these high walls. He would be better off going back to the top.

He was retracing his way up when he heard something. It was coming from somewhere above him. A thin piping, like someone playing a sad little tune.

Davey ran up the rest of the steps and turned into Harrow Lane. There was a boy sitting on the pavement a few yards away with his back against the wall and his legs stretched out. Davey thought he must be a street beggar, although he had no cap with him, no way of collecting the money. He was about Davey's age, perhaps a little younger, and was playing on a penny whistle.

The boy certainly looked like a beggar. His face was

27

thin and his skin showed white under a streaky film of grime. His feet were bare. His collarless shirt was grey and frayed. He wore cut-off men's trousers tied with rope round the waist. Davey wondered at his choice of pitch. There was nobody about . . .

The clear piping became louder, stranger, like some kind of calling. The boy's fingers fixed on one wild fine note and all the air about him seemed to shimmer. Davey had never heard such a beautiful tune, happy and sad at the same time. He found himself drawn towards it, almost as if he was being reeled in. He approached smiling, digging in his pocket for change, but the boy looked up from his playing, his eyes widening in surprise and fear. He struggled to his feet, backing away, large eyes dark in his pale face.

'It's OK,' Davey said, 'I'm not going to hurt you . . .'

The boy took the pipe out of his mouth and shook his head quickly from side to side. Davey's smile faltered. Maybe this kid was some kind of Care in the Community street crazy. Then he realised: the boy was not looking *at* him. His gaze was fixed on someone, or something *behind* him.

Whoever, whatever it was made no sound, but Davey could feel cold breath on the back of his neck.

'Hello.' The word purred close to his ear. 'You look lost.'

There were two of them, standing either side of him. Older than him, maybe sixteen or seventeen. They both wore ripped jeans and leather jackets. One of them had long fairish hair hanging down to his shoulders. The other was smaller, darker. He wore a stained baseball cap and was leaning heavily on a motorbike. A helmet swung from the handle bar. It would not be much use in an accident, Davey thought. The surface was roughened and scored; the visor shattered; the toughened fibreglass casing cracked like an eggshell.

'I – I was with some people,' Davey began to say. The way they looked at him made him nervous. Not exactly hostile, more predatory. He must have stumbled into their turf, their territory. 'I – I kind of got separated . . .'

'You with one of them Ghost Walk crews?'

'Yes. Haunts Tours.' Davey nodded. 'Do you know them?'

'You could say that.'

The blond one smiled and a sly look passed between the two older boys. The dark one sniggered as if at a private joke and pushed at the shattered helmet.

'Do you know how long they'll be?' asked Davey.

'That's hard to say. It depends.'

'On what?'

'Lots of things. They're a waste of time,' the blond boy flicked his hair back from his face. 'You want to come with us,' he grinned at his mate, his mouth twisting to match the greedy gleam in his eyes. 'We'll show you the *real* ghost city. We know where the action is.'

He moved closer. The skin on his face was a dirty grey-white, peppered and streaked with black all down one side. An ugly, crooked scar disappeared under his hair, a crudely stitched zig-zag from jaw to temple. His colourless eyes were unblinking, cold and fishy. His lips pulled back over teeth yellow and sharp, like animal fangs suddenly bared. His breath stank like something had died in his mouth. Davey did not like the look of him at all. He tried to break away, but a hand tightened on his arm, the fingers as hard and cold as bone. The other boy leaned the bike against the wall.

'Leave me alone!' Davey tried to keep his voice deep, but the words came out in a high frightened squeak that made both the youths snicker with laughter.

The more Davey struggled, the harder he was held and the more they laughed. Then suddenly, they changed. The second youth was moving in for the finish; they were tiring of the game.

Davey gave one more heave to get free and avoid the arms reaching out for him, when he felt someone else beside him. The boy who had been playing the whistle was staring up at the two older boys. His blue-black eyes were huge, too large for his thin bony face, his gaze steady and unblinking. He put the pipe to his mouth and blew again, one shrill clear note which escalated higher and higher, out of Davey's hearing.

'Shut that!' The blond one made a swipe for the whistle but the boy dodged back.

'Clear off, Govan,' the other one scowled. 'We saw him first!'

The boy Govan looked up at him, shaking his head.

'What are you going to do about it? You little runt!' Cold fingers tightened on Davey's neck. 'We'll deal with you just as soon as—'

'Hold it,' the dark one snapped.

'What?'

'Ssh!'

The two boys froze. Govan's head turned, cocked like a dog. All three were listening to a sound Davey could not hear. Then he heard it, too, echoing along the cobbled street, the steady thud of hoof beats.

Davey felt the grip on his throat relax. The other boy was already revving the bike.

'We're off to tell the Judge about this,' he yelled to Govan above the engine snarl. 'We'll get him – one way or another.'

'You and all,' the dark boy added as he scrambled on behind. 'You little . . .'

The threat was lost in choking smoke as the boys roared off. In the silence they left behind, the hoof beats were coming closer, echoing off the buildings, filling the narrow space between them. Davey remembered something about hoof beats, something Louise had said, but before he could do anything a huge black shape was towering over him. He cringed away to the side, afraid he would be trampled, but the horse wheeled and turned.

31

'What is your name, boy?' the rider demanded. 'And what are you doing here?'

'Davey. David Williams. I – I came with my sister. We kind of got separated.'

Before Davey could protest, or explain further, a strong arm reached down, hauling him up in front of the saddle. The horseman kicked his steed forward and sparks flew as iron-shod hooves clashed on the cobbles. He ducked, pushing Davey's head down, as they passed under the low creaking sign and into the yard of *The Seven Dials*.

6

'What do you think this is? *The Lion, the Witch and the Wardrobe*?' Kate said impatiently.

She was refusing to take her cousins' suggestion seriously. She'd forgotten how weird they could be, especially Elinor. Weirder than this place with its mirrors and purple drapes and pentagrams and stuff, and that was saying something. Weirder than Davey. Her brother was clearly not here but she was using the torch to check the corners, just to make sure.

'No,' Elinor replied. 'That was a wardrobe. This is a mirror. So it'd be more like *Alice Through the Looking Glass*.'

'It looks like it could be off a wardrobe, though,' Tom remarked, examining the large oval mirror.

'Whatever!' Kate rolled her eyes as she carried on her search. 'He's probably sitting out on the steps right now. I don't believe we're having this conversation! Things like that just do not happen!'

'Maybe,' Elinor stood next to her brother, head on one side. 'But you've got to admit it *is* strange . . .'

She looked at the mirror. The edges were still misted up but they bore the imprint of hands and the central section held a fuzzy outline of something which could have been a body. It was about Davey's size . . .

'That shape definitely wasn't there before.' Elinor stepped nearer. 'It looks like someone's gone right up and leaned against it.' she fitted her hands over the prints on the glass. 'Like this.'

'What are you doing, El?' Tom yelled. 'Come away from it!'

Kate whirled round, alerted by the sudden note of panic in his voice. 'What's the matter? What's all the fuss . . .'

She was talking to an empty room. In the time it took to turn, they had disappeared. Kate found herself quite alone. She blinked. Once. Twice. Unable to believe her eyes. She looked around, just to make sure. The room was empty. Her breath came fast, stirring the stale air and the hairs prickled up the back of her neck, as she went over to the mirror. Her palms were slick with sweat, slipping on the surface, as she placed them over the blurred hand shapes. They could be Davey's, she told herself, her hands were bigger than his . . .

The mirror must have fronted some kind of concealed entrance. When she got outside Tom and Elinor were waiting for her, but there was still no sign of Davey.

'We could split up,' Tom suggested. 'El and me can look down there.' He indicated the road at the bottom of the steps. 'While you go up to the top.'

'No,' Kate said quickly.

At first glance, everything seemed the same, but it was

not. There was something distinctly odd. The sky was a peculiar mix of gold and grey, and there was no city noise, no traffic rumble. No sound at all, in fact.

'No,' she repeated, the eerie atmosphere was beginning to get to her. 'I don't think that's a good idea. I think that we should stick together . . . Hang on,' she stopped to listen. 'What's that?'

They all looked up, relief spreading through them at the sound coming down the steps. Ordinary street noise heard in any town, any city; reassuringly familiar in all this strangeness; the deep-throated growl of a powerful motorbike.

7

Davey had been bundled into this empty room and told not to move. It was on the ground floor and smelt strange, of smoke and dust and age. It was cold. Faded panelling covered the walls and the floor was bare boards. A huge fireplace yawned around a black empty grate. The room had an unlived-in feeling, like the waiting room in some old-fashioned train station. Dusty diamond panes warped the world outside. Davey's eyes flicked up to the thick wooden sign hanging creaking in the windless street. Peeling gold paint described a series of circles with stars inside, like so many small compasses. Underneath, curly writing read: *The Seven Dials*. Davey stood looking out. Pinching himself didn't work, it just left white finger marks and hurt. Yet the whole thing had a dream-like feeling . . . Davey shook his head, he was having difficulty thinking about it. His mind kept drifting as though he was in shock. His numbed brain had so far failed all attempts to make sense of what was happening to him, let alone tell him what to do.

'Hello,' a voice said, young, light and very precise. 'I am Elizabeth. Elizabeth Hamilton. What's your name?'

Davey turned to find a girl of about Kate's age staring at

him. She stood, head on one side, regarding him with grave grey eyes. Her long dark hair hung loose, curling and waving past her shoulders. She was wearing an old-fashioned costume: a wide grey skirt and fitted jacket and tight button boots laced up to her knees.

'David,' he replied, 'but my friends call me Davey.'

'I had better call you David, then. Because we do not know each other.'

Davey did not reply. Unsure what to make of this strange girl, or any of the other people he had so far encountered, he could think of nothing to say. The girl was deadly pale, as white as Govan and those boys with the motorbike, and then there was the way she was dressed. There could be a good reason for that, the thought suddenly occurred to him. She could be in a pageant, or going to a fancy dress as Alice, or maybe she was part of a film crew . . .

Of course! That would fit the horseman, too! He'd had old-fashioned clothes on. That's why they were all in period costume, and this room – it was part of a film set. The theory had holes in it, did not make total sense but, Davey grinned, it made more sense than any of his other theories. This idea gave him new confidence to speak to her.

'Who are you?'

'Elizabeth Hamilton. I just told you.'

'No, I mean, this is a film, right? Who are you playing in it?'

'Film?' Elizabeth frowned as if she'd never heard of such a thing. 'Playing? I don't understand.'

'OK. OK. So it isn't a film.' Davey racked his brains for a different explanation. 'I know, it's one of those Crime Night evenings where people dress up in period costume, act things out – murders and stuff like that.'

'Period costume.' She looked down at her clothes. 'No. This is what I always wear. And I'm not acting. As for murder . . . I'm sorry, I still don't understand . . .'

That makes two of us, Davey thought, and lapsed into silence.

Elizabeth wondered if she ought to tell him, or wait for him to ask her. Tell him what? That he was the only living, breathing human being in a world of ghosts? He was unlikely to believe her and there was something about this encounter that she would like to extend. He thought she was a real person. She liked that. It made her feel more . . . substantial. She watched him for a moment, studying the emotions flickering across his face. He reminded her of her brother. Harry was younger, of course, by several years, but he and this boy shared the same stocky build, the same dark colouring, the same common sense, the same way of hiding their fear under layers of stubbornness. 'A good chap to have in your corner', that's what Father had said about Harry. She had not thought of Harry in a very long time. A feeling she had almost forgotten wrenched deep down inside her. Pain. A sense of loss. Something forever gone.

'What's the matter?' Davey asked, he had never seen such sadness on a human face before.

'Nothing. You just remind me of someone.'

'Who?'

'Harry. He was – is – my brother. It is of no matter.'

'Was? Is? You don't sound sure.'

'How can I be?' she replied, almost fiercely. 'Time here runs differently.' She turned away from him, her voice low and bitter.

'Here.' Davey pulled a grubby hanky from his pocket. She looked as if she was about to cry.

Elizabeth stared at the offered handkerchief, uncomprehending, and then she laughed. Her laugh was like her voice, high and light, like a silvery wind chime.

'Ghosts don't cry.'

'Oh, right,' Davey found himself joining in. 'I get it now. I understand. It's not a Crime Night thing. You dress up as ghosts to scare the tourists on the Ghost Walks . . .'

Her laughing stopped, as if someone had switched it off.

'No. I don't think you do. Understand, I mean.' She frowned again, her pale face serious. 'I really *am* a ghost. So is Govan, and the man who brought you here.'

'How about the boys on motorbikes, the ones he saved me from?' Davey asked, struggling to keep afloat the rafts of reason his mind had built for itself. 'They were dressed in modern clothes – in jeans and leathers and baseball caps . . .'

'They are the Recent Dead. Not all ghosts are ancient, you know. Not all of them died a long time ago. They could have died yesterday. Today . . .'

Davey suddenly felt faint. He'd seen the film *Ghost*. He could feel the blood beating in his head. He cleared his throat.

'What about me? Does that mean . . . ? Am I . . . ?'

'A ghost?' She shook her head. 'No. I can feel your blood heat from here. See your skin colour next to mine.' She came over and put a small cold hand on his. It was blanched white, almost transparent in its thinness. 'You are still alive.'

'So you're not acting, and I'm not a ghost, but I still don't understand . . .' Davey's brown eyes appealed to her for help. 'What exactly is going on here?'

'I don't know. Somehow you have wandered from your world into ours. It happens sometimes. You are just lucky that Govan found you and sought help.'

'But how do I get back?' Davey asked, looking about, trying to control his sudden surging panic.

'It very rarely happens . . .' She bit her lip. 'I simply have no idea. But I don't think it will be easy. Jack might know . . .'

'Who's Jack?'

'Jack Cade. The man who brought you here.'

'The highwayman?'

'Why, yes. Have you heard of him?'

'Yes,' Davey swallowed. 'I – I did hear him mentioned.'

'Which reminds me.' her smooth marble brow contracted in a frown. 'He should be back by now . . .'

She went to the door, but it opened before she could reach it. Another young woman came into the room, older than Elizabeth, in her early twenties. A full-sleeved white blouse billowed from under her tightly-laced bodice and her long skirt covered her ankles. Her dark hair was tied back, tucked under a red kerchief. She was pretty with a clear featured face and eyes as bright and black as Govan's.

'Who are you?' Davey blurted out. How many people were there here?

'I could ask the same of you. I'm Polly Martin.'

Polly Martin. Jack Cade. *The Seven Dials*. The pounding hooves. Davey felt weak, light headed. This was a ghost story coming to life . . .

'Where *is* Jack?'

Polly sounded anxious. She had gone over to the window and was peering through the thick distorting glass into the street outside.

'Were you alone?'

'Excuse me?' Davey suddenly realised she was talking to him.

'When you came here. Were you on your own?'

'No. I was with other people . . .'

'He was with one of the Ghost Walk crews,' Elizabeth supplied.

'These others?' Polly persisted. 'Might you have been missed?'

'I was with my sister and my cousins . . .'

'Might they have followed you? Might they have found a way through also?'

'I don't know. I guess it's possible . . .'

'Let's hope for their sakes that they did not.'

'Polly?' Elizabeth looked in alarm at the older woman. 'What can you see?'

Polly turned back from the window, arms folded, frown deepening.

'The Black Sentinels are out searching the streets.' She nodded towards Davey. 'We must get him away from here.'

'Shouldn't we wait . . .'

'There is no time. Take him through to next door. Quickly. Quickly! I'll stay in case Jack comes back . . .'

'And if he doesn't?'

Polly did not answer. Her eyes were trained on what was happening outside. Dark shadows were approaching, crowding the windows, sucking out the light. Black shapes were probing the diamond panes, slanting into the room like long fingers of solid darkness.

Davey did not have to know what these Black Sentinels were, he could sense their evil from here. Elizabeth took

42

his hand and indicated that he should step backwards. They crept towards the door with careful quiet tread. This was no time for questions. Davey moved with silent stealth, as if he himself was a spectre.

8

Kate went towards the motorbike sound, running up Keeper's Steps, followed by Tom and Elinor, but when they got to the top, there was no sign of anyone.

'Where can he be?' Kate looked up and down a deserted Harrow Lane, searching for her brother, fear and guilt churning inside her.

'We'll find him.' Tom put his hand on her shoulder. 'Don't worry.'

'Maybe he went back to the Market Square,' Elinor suggested. 'Maybe he headed back the way we came.'

'Could have, I suppose,' Kate muttered doubtfully, unwilling to accept hope too soon.

'And which way's that?' Tom asked, gazing about.

'I thought we came through there.' Elinor pointed. 'That little alley.'

'And I thought we came down there.' Tom waved to a wider street off to the right. 'But I remember going past a row of, like, craft shops and that.' He frowned. 'It doesn't look the same, somehow . . .'

Kate and Elinor could see what he meant. The way the roads met, the buildings either side, even the surface beneath their feet, all seemed different. Harrow Lane was rutted, cut with grooves left by heavy, narrow-wheeled traffic. Grass grew up the middle of it, dried mud stood in ridges. Although it was hard to recall exactly what it had looked like before, it had not been like this.

Kate shivered, pulling her sweater around her. The sun was going down early. Night was falling quickly. What else could account for the shadows gathering, gliding up the steps behind them, thickening like black mist at either end of the street?

A horse neighed and whinnied. They turned to see a horseman cantering towards them, a barefoot boy trotting by his side, holding on to the horse's bridle. The man brought his mount up short, and sat tall in the saddle, gazing down at them. He was youngish, with handsome hawk-like features and long black hair curling past his shoulders. He wore a black scarf twisted round his neck, a coat of wine-red velvet over a loose white shirt, and wide breeches tucked into high leather boots. An old-fashioned pistol stuck out from his wide belt and a short sword, or long dagger, hung in a scabbard by his side.

'Do you have a brother?' he asked. 'David Williams?'

'Yes! Do you know where he is?' The man nodded and Kate smiled up at him, relief sweeping away any fear of strangeness. 'Can you take us to him?'

The man nodded again, wheeling his horse around.

'Keep close. Two this side, one that side with Govan. When I spur the horse run as if your life depended on it.'

'Why should we?' Tom asked, suspicious.

45

'If you want to see him again, you have no choice.'

'Is he in danger?'

'I speak not of him,' the horseman replied. Kate was suddenly aware of the shadows gathering on every side. The horse reared as the sharp spur bit into its flank. 'Stay close to me.'

The horseman led them through a maze of back ways and alleys, through yards and over fences, and into the yard of *The Seven Dials*.

'Jack Cade at your service,' he said as he dismounted.

'The highwayman?' Kate looked at the others.

'Yes,' Jack smiled, teeth white against his black moustache. 'Have you heard of me?'

'Kind of,' Tom mumbled.

'And you are?'

'Tom. Tom Lynn. This is my sister, Elinor . . .'

'And I'm Kate, Davey's sister. Where is he?'

'In here.' Jack opened the door on an empty room. 'At least he was when I left, with strict instructions not to move . . .' It was Jack's turn to look puzzled and not a little worried. He stepped away from the door and began shouting, 'Polly! Elizabeth!' The worry on his face turning to real apprehension. 'Go and find them, Govan.'

'What is this place?' Tom looked round the cold dusty room. 'I don't understand what's going on here.'

'This is the inn of *The Seven Dials*.'

'That's impossible.' Tom shook his head. 'I remember walking past it. It's a tourist information office!'

'In your world, yes. But we are not in your world now.'

'I don't understand . . .' Tom paused. He could not go on saying that. He looked at the others. They were as confused as he was. 'Excuse me, Mr Cade—'

'Jack. You can call me Jack.'

'Right, Jack. Before we go any further, before anything else happens, I want you to tell me something. I mean, is it possible that, that you could be . . .'

'A ghost?' Jack's grin widened. 'Most assuredly. That's what I am.'

'OK. OK,' Tom stopped to consider. 'In that case, how did we get here?'

'I do not know. Except it is Midsummer's Eve, a time of powerful magic when the barrier between your world and ours grows thin. There are places, special places, where it is possible to move from one world to another. You must have stumbled upon such a one and now you are in another time altogether. Here *we* are real and *you* are the ghosts.'

'Are there more?' Elinor asked. 'More than just you?'

'Of course! Ghosts are divided into groups – crews – and each crew has its own territory. You find yourselves in mine. Govan, Polly and Elizabeth are my crew. We are just one, there are many more in the city.'

'Are they . . .' Elinor could feel the hairs creeping up the back of her neck. 'These others – are they dangerous?'

'Not all of them, but some undoubtedly are. They prize the living very highly. There are those who long to return to the world that they have left, they would steal your living breath . . .'

'I thought ghosts couldn't hurt you,' Tom said defiantly. He did not like people scaring his sister.

'I don't know who told you that. Not so much in your world, perhaps. But you are in their world now, don't you understand? No one died well here.' Jack's face twisted in anger. 'No one died safe in their bed after living out three score years and ten. Look.' He pulled the scarf away from his neck and held his head high. An ugly black mark, thick and ribbed, extended round from each ear, meeting below the chin. 'I bear the mark of the hanged man. Each of us bears the scars—'

'Hush, Jack.' A woman's voice sounded from the door. 'You will frighten them.'

'So they should be frightened. Very frightened—'

'What is the point of that?' The woman stepped forward, holding up a hand for his silence. 'I am Polly. Polly Martin. You must be Kate?' Kate nodded. 'Your brother is safe—'

'Where is he?'

'Next door with Elizabeth, another of our crew. Come along. We will do our best to get you back.'

'How do we know we can trust you?' Tom asked,

reluctant to leave without knowing where they were going.

'Shut up, Tom!' Kate whispered. 'What choice do we have?'

The young woman smiled. 'We have no love for the Sentinels or their master. We will help you return to your own world, I promise you.'

'Have the Sentinels been here?' Jack asked.

Polly nodded. 'And gone. But they will return, we can be sure of that.'

'Who are these Sentinels?' Kate demanded. 'What can they do?'

'They are like watchmen, guarding the boundary between our world and yours. If they find a breach, they track down the trespassers and take them to the Judge. The Judge controls the whole city and all of us, or thinks he does. He holds the Book of Possibilities which contains the name and history of every ghost in the city.'

'Who's the Judge? What will he do to us?'

'He was, is, an evil man. It is best not to speak too long of him. He – he has special uses for the living. If he seizes you,' she shuddered slightly, 'he will punish us and any hope of your escape would be gone for ever.'

'How *can* we escape? How can we get away?'

Polly looked at Jack. 'We must get them to the Blind Fiddler.'

'If we can find him.' Jack frowned. 'That could be difficult. And dangerous. For us as much as for them.'

'We must,' Polly said simply. 'We are committed now. The Sentinels will be back . . .'

'These Sentinels,' Kate asked, 'are they ghosts like you?'

'Not exactly. They are hard to describe. Dark pillars without light. Form without substance. Shadows adrift from the body which cast them. They do not see with their eyes. They have other senses. They hunt with silent thoroughness . . .'

'Do they . . .'

'We can waste no more time on explanations.' Jack cut off Kate's questioning. 'We must seek the Blind Fiddler, to see if he cannot return you to your own world.' He turned to Polly. 'Tonight there will be a Gathering. We will take the smugglers' route through the tunnels to the Market Square and see if we can get word of him there. Go and fetch Elizabeth and the boy.'

There was a small door cut into the panelling at the side of the huge fireplace. Jack went over to it now and beckoned for the others to follow. In front of him lay a flight of narrow steep steps disappearing down into the black depths of the cellars.

At the top, Kate hesitated and turned back.

'I want to wait here for Davey.'

'There is no time.' Polly urged her forward. 'I will bring him to you.'

'What if you can't?' Kate's eyes glanced to the window, to the shadows gathering in the street outside.

'If we become separated for any reason,' Polly smiled

down, anxious to reassure the girl, 'we will meet you in the Market Square, on the south side of the cathedral.'

'You promise?'

'We will be there.'

9

Davey and Elizabeth sat waiting in the basement next door. Time here might run differently, but it seemed to be stretching into infinity. Conversation was difficult, full of false starts and blind alleys. Davey hoped that Polly would not be long.

'How did you get here, then?' he asked Elizabeth. 'What happened to you?'

She went over to the window, looking up to the street above.

'I was killed outside here. Right on those cobbles. Trampled by a horse. The poor thing had been startled by a horseless carriage.' She turned to him with a slight smile. 'I was one of the first casualties of the internal combustion engine.'

'What about Polly?'

'She was shot. Jack was hanged. Each of them bears the marks, black marks on the skin, as evidence of their fatal injury.'

'Ugh, that's awful!' Davey exclaimed, his eyes widening with horror.

'They fade in time,' Elizabeth replied, matter-of-factly, as if she was talking about operation scars.

'You too?' Davey asked with a shudder.

She shook her dark curls. 'I am unmarked. My injuries were all internal.'

He did not know if he should be, but Davey was glad. She was so pretty and, although it sounded silly, so alive somehow. Not ghost-like at all. She seemed like a *real* girl. He did not like to think about her being all marked and scarred about.

'How come you are all together in one place, if you're from different times?' Davey asked, then he added something else that had been on his mind. 'Why doesn't everybody become a ghost?'

The light died from her grey eyes; she suddenly looked much older than her apparent years and her small heart-shaped face became sombre and thoughtful.

'People seemed to stay about the place of their death. Jack was taken from here. I was killed outside. Polly was murdered. As for why we are ghosts?' She shrugged. 'Who knows? Except as Jack says, no one died well or safe in their beds . . .'

'What about Govan?'

'We can't be sure. He just turned up one day. There are no marks upon his body and he can't tell us what happened to him because he can't talk.' She paused and looked away, giving Davey the distinct feeling that she was hiding something. When she spoke again it was to change the subject.

'Being a ghost isn't all gloom and misery, you know. We have fun sometimes, especially Govan and I.'

'Oh? Like how?'

'Well, take this place.' She gestured round. 'This room.'

'What about it?'

'It is not always as you see it now. Sometimes it is different. It is as if there are two worlds existing in the same space but parallel to each other. This place, for example, is also a tea room full of people dressed in clothes of a different age.'

'No kidding!' Davey leaned forward, excited. 'That's what it is! Now, I mean. In my time. When the place goes like that, what happens then?'

'Govan and I *haunt* it. We jog elbows and knock tea cups; we make things appear and disappear. Sometimes people even *see* us.' Elizabeth's grey eyes sparkled like ice in sunlight. 'It is such a *lark*, Davey. You have no idea.'

Davey nodded, his own dark eyes shining with excitement. Being a ghost could have real potential. He could see that.

'If that were to happen, if the place were to go that way, like right now – would I be a ghost, too?'

'Such a thing has never occurred before, I have no idea . . .'

'Can you make it happen, though? Could you make it happen now?'

'I don't know.' She frowned, then gave a mischievous grin. 'But I could try.'

Elizabeth shut her eyes and fell silent. She sat motionless, hands clasped in her lap, chin resting on her chest. Watching her, Davey thought that she had fallen asleep. She stayed like that for a long time. So long, that Davey was convinced nothing was going to happen, when suddenly the light in the room changed. The windows grew curtains, tables and chairs formed out of thin air, and the room was filled with the muffled chatter of many voices, the chink of china.

Elizabeth was sitting in a chair by the window. She seemed very solid, but Davey nearly called out a warning: a fat lady was about to sit on top of her. Just in time, Elizabeth stood up, gliding through her. The woman looked from side to side and shuddered slightly, pulling her coat in against a sudden chill, before shaking her head and picking up a menu.

Davey could see what Elizabeth meant about the worlds being parallel. When he looked down, his own feet were not there. They had disappeared through the floor. He was standing on a different level. The living were like ghosts. All the way up the café, the people were bright outlines sketched on the air, like jellyfish in water.

'Now comes the fun,' Elizabeth whispered in his ear. 'We'll start with the woman who nearly sat on me.'

Elizabeth leaned towards the woman and blew, her breath riffling the pages of the menu. The woman smoothed them, and then smoothed them again. Finally she summoned a waitress and demanded to be moved, complaining about the fierce draught from the window.

Davey thought he would have a go himself. Nothing spectacular. Just knocking a menu over. He hovered near two women just settling down to tea and gateaux. He tried but nothing happened. The menu stayed upright, propped open on the table. He stepped back disappointed: a first haunt failure.

'Not like that.' Elizabeth had come back from where she had been encouraging a man to spill tea into his lap. 'You can't do things just with your hands. Look.' She went to pick up a salt shaker and her hand went straight through it. 'You must use thought, too. Imagine the action at the same time, kind of *will* it to happen, and then it should work. See?'

This time he was successful. The cruet fell over, spilling salt across the table. One woman apologised for her clumsiness, the other took a pinch of salt and threw it over her shoulder. Elizabeth quickly pulled Davey out of the way.

'Watch out! Salt can affect us badly. You have a try now. Go on. Nothing too dramatic, though,' she warned, 'no flying cream cakes or anything like that.'

'Why not?' Davey asked, disappointed. Custard pies were exactly what he had in mind.

'We are not supposed to interfere directly with the living. Something like that would be too obvious. It would create all kinds of fuss and hullabaloo and that would alerts other ghost crews, not to mention the Black Sentinels. It might even invite the interest of human psychics who can see us. Some leave us alone, but others set themselves up as ghost-hunters. And that would make us extremely unpopular. Their busybody poking about can wreak havoc in the city. So,' she wagged her finger at him, 'be warned: don't do anything silly.'

Davey did as she said and contented himself with knocking a few things over, jogging the odd elbow or two. Still, this was fun in itself, hearing people apologise to each other, watching them wipe themselves down. None of them guessed the source of the chaos. They blamed themselves, each other, the waitress. None of them even came close, or ever would have, if it had not been for the last customer.

A woman came in, stern-looking, with strong features and a prominent hawk-like nose. Her black hair was streaked at the front with white, combed back and fixed behind with a slide. She was tall and slim, dressed in a flowery blouse and long summer skirt. She swept down the stairs with her friend, but did not make her way to a seat. She stood at the door, black eyes darting round, thin nostrils flaring as if she was scenting the air. Her face grew pale and she pulled her friend to her side, whispering urgently in her ear.

'I can feel something,' she said with a shiver. 'There's something, or someone, active here.'

Then she looked round again. 'One there, a girl,' she said, pointing to where Elizabeth was standing by the wall. 'And one over there.' Her finger came to a wavering rest at the sweet trolley where Davey was interfering with the puddings: sprinkling salt, squashing icing, spilling cream. 'A boy, I think it is, but,' she put a hand to her pale lips, 'he looks wrong to me, funny somehow.' She plucked at her friend's arm. 'There is an unpleasant atmosphere – obviously renewed activity here. I'd better inform the Society.'

The waitress came over to take them to a table.

'Tell me, my dear,' Davey heard the woman say. 'Have you had anything strange going on here recently?'

'Well,' the young waitress looked taken aback, 'odd you should say that because things *have* been happening. I mean, only just now, I had a tray of cakes go over and I swear there was no one even near. And that man over there had practically a whole cup of tea dumped in his lap. And Josie's noticed things upstairs, haven't you, Josie?'

The lady nodded and smiled as another waitress came over and added her tale. The stories went on and on. Once people started, there was no stopping them.

'We must go,' Elizabeth whispered in Davey's ear.

'Why? This is fun.'

'That woman over there? The one with the white streak in her hair? She's a medium. She can see us.'

Davey did not have time to ask more. Elizabeth collected him by the shoulder and took him backwards out of the room one step at a time. The lady watched them; her dark, hooded eyes marking their retreat. She was a psychic of some reputation and ghosts of all kinds were her sworn enemies.

10

The cellars were cold and the small rooms smelt of soot; coal crunched underfoot. At first, it was so completely dark that Kate sensed rather than saw the space around her, only Tom breathing near her ear told her she was not alone. Gradually her eyes adjusted to the relative absence of light until she could see Jack standing close, the whites of his eyes gleaming, his shirt glimmering under his dark coat. The tension was getting to her. Waiting time weighed heavy. She had the uncomfortable feeling that Davey should have joined them by now.

'Excuse me,' she whispered up to the highwayman. 'But shouldn't they be here?'

Jack frowned. He had been thinking the same thing.

'What happens if they don't come? I mean, what happens . . .'

Kate's words were cut off. By Jack's side, Govan made a high thin mewing sound. His black eyes glittered huge with fear and under its streaky layer of dirt, his face was bleached of colour. He pulled at Jack's coat sleeve. His other arm pointed over to the far end of the room and up at the ceiling.

Jack put a finger to his lips. From the floor above came the sound of a slow dragging shuffle. What kind of thing made a sound like that? Nothing that was human, or had ever drawn breath. Along the furthest wall darkness seemed to be gathering, filtering through the floorboards, drifting down like black sand. Kate watched, fascinated as the blackness collected, clotting into clumps of formless mass which began to take on shape . . .

'Stand still!' Jack ordered and pressed a lever to the side. Unseen machinery whirred into action and the whole section of stone began a slow grinding turn, taking them from the cellar round to the smugglers' tunnels which ran from the inn down to the river.

Above them, Polly retreated from the inky mass of Sentinels swarming through the ground floor rooms. Her way to Jack was blocked. She hurried up the stairs, crossed through to the house next door and silently descended the stairs to the basement. Elizabeth and Davey would be waiting there. It was too late to join the others. They would have to find their own way to the Market Square and pray to all meet at the Gathering.

Kate wanted to stay and wait for the others to come.

'They won't come now,' Jack said, anxious to get away from the secret door to the cellar.

'Why not?' Kate demanded stubbornly.

'Because the way is blocked by the Sentinels. They will have to take another route. Don't worry.' His attitude softened a little as he realised how upset she was. 'Your brother will be safe with Polly. She is kind and sensible; she will look after him. And she is canny. She knows the city better than any. She will know where to go and what to do. It is probably safer if we go different ways.'

He took a torch from an iron bracket set in to the wall. Flint sparked on metal and a sputtering orange flame flared up, making the shadows leap and dance up the wall.

'Come on. The quicker we get started, the quicker we can meet in the Market Square and find the Blind Fiddler.'

'Excuse me,' Elinor whispered up to the highwayman. 'Can you tell me something?'

'If I can.'

'Who is this Blind Fiddler person? And how can he help us?'

'The Fiddler is wise in the ways of the city. Some say that, in his living days, he was a very great magician, steeped in learning and secret knowledge. Tonight he is with the Host in the Great Hall. It is Midsummer, a special day for them. One of their great loves is music and he plays better than even their musicians.'

'Who are the Host?' Kate asked nervously. She felt Govan stir by her side and tense with fear.

'I'm not sure what you would call them,' Jack replied. 'They have different names in different places, some call them the Sidhe, some the Unseelie Court. They are not ghosts at all. They have never been human. They are Other and can never be too much avoided. They never, under any circumstances, favour humankind – living or dead. They hold the living in especial contempt and hatred. The Blind Fiddler is with them – at the Court of their leader, the Old Grey Man, and his daughter. A place even the dead dare not enter. They are the worst, the worst of the worst, but that is where we must go if we are to find him. He is the only one who knows the magic that opens the way between the worlds. The Blind Fiddler knows the portals, he will know where to take you, but even then,' he paused, 'it is only fair to warn you, there is no guarantee . . .'

'Of what? He *can* get us back . . . ?'

'It's not that – it's just how much time has elapsed since you left.' Jack bit his lip. 'It could be seconds, it could be centuries . . .'

'Like Rip Van Winkle, you mean?' Tom commented sceptically. 'Oh, come on!'

'It is not a fit subject for mirth,' Jack Cade snapped, annoyed at this interruption. 'Time runs differently here. There is a distinct possibility that you will return to find your loved ones long dead.'

'But surely—'

'Ssh, Tom.' Elinor put her hand on his arm. 'This is his world. We have to listen. What could happen?' She looked up at the highwayman. 'What could happen to us then, when we do get back?'

'You might find that no time has gone at all, or . . .'

'Or?'

'Or you could turn to dust in an eye's twinkling. Now,' he urged them forward, 'we must go on.'

The smell of stone and the darkness thickening in front of them reminded Kate of the plague streets that they had visited on the Haunts Tour. What if we never come out? She thought as she looked into the brick-bound blackness beyond the sickly torchlight. Finding Davey again might be the least of their worries. She remembered what that girl, Louise, had said about this being the true ghost city, the realm of the dead. Kate swallowed hard as she followed Jack into the cold damp space. His torch cast unsteady shadows on rough walls and her heart beat as hollow as their footsteps on the smooth stone floor as she considered the alternative fates on offer to them: to stay here for ever, or turn to dust.

Her cousins didn't say anything, but she knew they were thinking the same thing. Elinor squeezed her hand. Tom stared straight ahead, a little knot of doubt and worry cramping his forehead.

There was a scraping scuffling sound from further down the tunnel and the torchlight seemed to waver, as from a sudden gust of wind.

'Are there – are there ghosts and things down here, too?' Elinor said.

Jack nodded. 'But don't worry. Most of those we meet will be locked in their time so they will probably not even notice you. To ghosts the living are invisible, just as we are in your world.'

'What if they do notice us?' Tom asked.

'Down here, we are most likely to meet smugglers. They are my good friends, so we should be all right with them, but just to be safe, do not speak or react in any way. Do not even move. Leave any talking to me. Do you understand?'

They nodded.

'Good. Very good. This tunnel branches and leads to other hidden ways, and yet more hidden ways. The whole city is riddled with underground passages so it is important that you stay close, do not on any account go wandering off. If you do get separated, stay where you are. Govan will find you. We will try to avoid the most dangerous areas, but from here on you must obey my every command. It may be a matter of life or death.'

The scuffling sound was getting louder, turning into the booming rattle of barrels being rolled along the ground.

Jack put up a hand, signalling them to halt. Rough voices, muttering and cursing, accompanied the clang of metal on stone. With a sweep of his arm, he indicated for them to get back. They shrank against the dripping brick wall, eyes trained on the curving length of the tunnel, fixed at a point where the flickering light of many torches showed and columns of men came into view.

The men marched along the tunnel rolling big barrels between them. They did not look like Kate's idea of smugglers, they were grim faced and uniformed.

'Revenue men!' Jack Cade hissed. 'If they catch me, I'm a dead man!'

'I thought you were anyway,' Tom said.

'Here you can die more than once.' Jack pulled at the scarf round his neck as though it was choking him. 'That is one of the special delights of the place. We must retrace our steps. There is a side tunnel a little way back from here. I'd thought not to use it, except in direst emergency but . . .' he paused, easing the scarf again. 'Govan will take the lead.'

He passed the boy the torch and they retreated back the way they had come. The side tunnel was small. The walls were not brick, they were stone, carved from the living rock. Quarried from ancient times, this whole area was honeycombed; much of the old city had been built with stone from here. The opening was low and squat, gaping like a dark mouth fringed by dripping slime and black moss. The other tunnels had been cold, damp, uncomfortable, but this was different. Even Govan seemed reluctant to enter. As he dipped his torch towards the entrance, it flickered and dimmed blue as if caught by the breath of something evil.

11

Many metres above them, Polly was leading Davey and Elizabeth along the length of Quarry Street. When Davey asked where they were going, Polly had replied, 'To meet your cousins and sister. They are with Jack and they go to find the Blind Fiddler. He is the only one who can get you out of here.' Now they walked in silence. It was safer that way and Polly and Elizabeth were not speaking. Polly was furious about the tea shop escapade. Going into the world of the living was dangerous at the best of times. Watchers on both sides could be alerted. And now? At a time like this? With the Sentinels in the very same row? For the sake of a silly jape? Foolish to the point of lunacy.

Elizabeth was not speaking to Davey, either. She seemed lost in her own thoughts; distant and withdrawn again after they had been getting on so well. She blamed him for getting her into trouble with Polly and that was unfair since the whole thing had been her idea. Davey knew she blamed him for Polly finding out. All he'd done was tell her about the fun they'd had. How was he to know that Polly would really freak out? Polly did not know about the woman who had seen them, the medium. Elizabeth had been careful to miss her out of the account and Davey thought it best not to mention her. He did not want to suffer more of Elizabeth's displeasure, even if they had done no harm that he could see. Davey failed to understand what the fuss was all about. And why were they going so slowly? There was no one around. The streets seemed utterly deserted. Davey wondered where the others were, Kate, Tom and Elinor. At first, knowing they were here had made him feel less lonely, but now he was scared for them, too.

It was night-time in Ghost City, or seemed to be. The sky was dark but showed no moon, no stars – yet it was not quite pitch-black. Davey had the feeling that it was always like that: never quite dark, never quite light. Never quite day, never quite night. Elizabeth had said time runs differently here. Davey wondered who controlled the 'dimmer switch'.

Every now and then, the world seemed to wobble, take on a definite shimmer. When that happened it was possible to see two worlds existing together. Cobblestones and pavement; parked cars and carriages; traffic lights and hitching posts; a zebra crossing strewn with straw and horse dung. One minute a row of houses were shuttered and dark, just like two hundred years ago, and the next they were covered in estate agents' boards, had signs like Citizens' Advice Bureau outside and Legal Aid stickers in the window. It was like a hologram, one ghostly scene swapping places with another in eerie 3D.

The shimmering, the thing Davey found interesting, was beginning to worry Polly. It hinted at strange happenings, an ominous instability. Also it did seem extremely quiet. In one way, deserted streets were good. Their journey went unchallenged and they could make good progress. No one being around suited their purposes. Especially here. She looked about. Quarry Street took them near the Judge's House and his crews were particularly dangerous. Polly had met the Judge only once, but like everyone else in the city she knew and feared his reputation. A man of great learning, in life he had been a sorcerer, so they said, a black magician in league with the Devil. He had been hanged for witchcraft and well deserved his fate. A true follower of the ways of evil, he now used his knowledge to control the City of the Dead.

Polly paused on the corner where four roads met. The silence was unreal, even for this place. No crew challenged them. Nothing stirred. There was no sound anywhere. She stood for a moment, her heart weighing heavy, doubts welling up inside her about Jack and the rest of the crew. There were many hazards underground. What if they became trapped? Caught by the Sentinels' underground cadres? Even if they escaped them, they might well find themselves in the Plague Quarter and overground crews were far from welcome in the Cairncross. The ghosts down there, caught up in their own frenzied misery, were apt to turn on outsiders, tearing them to pieces.

What if Jack and the others were not at the meeting place in the square beside the cathedral? How long should they wait for them? What if they never arrived?

Polly turned with a sigh and put these concerns to the back of her mind. Time enough to worry later. They were not there themselves yet. There was the Gathering

12

'Quickly now!' Jack hissed. 'Or they will be upon us.'

Govan glanced back, the Revenue men were advancing apace. They had no choice but to enter the tunnel. He thrust the light forward, the bluish flame illuminated a small space immediately in front of him. All the rest was blackness.

The rough-hewn walls were low, squat. Only Govan could walk upright. He went ahead, holding the torch, with Kate, Elinor and Tom crouching behind and Jack bent almost double.

Govan led them on, stopping at every branching turn, snuffing the air like a dog to seek the safest way. There were presences down here, too. The poisoned malice of centuries had drained down to this level. Inhabitants of forgotten burial vaults, dungeon masters and evil knights; those buried without the blessing of the church; suicides, murderers, these were spectres sent to haunt these underground places. They had no love for the daylight crews, even those of their own kind. Their job was to keep order here below. These were the Black Sentinels' underground troops.

Govan stopped so suddenly that Kate almost fell over him. He indicated urgently: Go back! Go back! Kate could see nothing but a mere thickening in the darkness ahead of them, then the light he was holding began to burn blue again and grow dim. The blackness in front seemed to solidify as the light died, separating into individual figures, each one robed and hooded. She heard a hissing, a mass intake of breath, and then a skittering as they began to move forward, like many dry sticks clicking and rubbing together.

'Thrust the torch towards them, Govan,' Jack whispered urgently, 'they do not like the light.'

Jack drew his sword and pistol, ready to stand and fight. Not that there would be much point. The torch was already burning low and Sentinels were immune to blade and bullet. He peered forward, trying to see past the flame Govan held. They were here in such numbers. Down here, Sentinels usually went alone, or in pairs, but here was a whole mass of them. The word must have come down from their master in the world above. They were hunting, sniffing and scenting the air in front of them, searching for Jack and his crew.

'There's another entrance up there.' Jack pointed along the tunnel. 'If we can hold them off long enough . . .'

Govan waved the torch from side to side, but the flame was failing badly now. The Sentinels were edging forward and there was no way round them, they stood solid from wall to wall. They were near enough for Kate to catch the greenish gleam of skull-like faces. Suddenly she remembered the torch in her pocket.

'Would this be any help?' She snapped on the bright halogen beam and aimed it at the one right at the front.

The lead Sentinel gasped and threw up its arms. Kate felt her grip falter as wide sleeves fell back to show white bone in hanging folds of leprous skin. She would have dropped the torch if Tom had not come to help her. Together they played the torch across the whole front line. The creatures had never confronted such a powerfully concentrated source of light before. In their haste to cringe away, they knocked into those behind, rank after rank collapsing back. Govan threw his torch into the confusion, aiming for the middle of the heaving mass. In the tightly-packed space fire spread quickly, consuming the surface blackness to expose helplessly writhing bone and skin.

'I've rarely seen such a rout.' Jack grinned his satisfaction once they had put distance between themselves and what was left of the Sentinels. 'That is a device of rare power you have there, Mistress Kate.'

'It's a torch.' Kate held it up to show him. 'It has energy inside. You can't use it all the time or the power in it dies. I think I'd better turn it off now,' she added. 'We might need it for later.'

'Hmm.' Jack was no longer smiling. 'Where we are going, I'd say that was more than likely.'

★   ★   ★

They were in a square-shaped tunnel, unlike any of the ones they had been in before. There was wood set into the walls. It was no longer completely dark. Up ahead light showed, grey and weak, as if obscured by mist or smoke. It was wet under foot. Mud squelched and sucked at their feet and the path was slippery. A smell like rotting vegetables oozed towards them, growing stronger as the tunnel widened towards an opening.

'I'd thought to avoid this warren of misery,' Jack said, 'but it seems we have no choice. Do not speak to anyone,' he warned. 'Look neither left nor right, but straight ahead. As I said before, you are the ghosts here, so with any luck none will see you. As for Govan and me.' He shrugged. 'Most folk here are too far sunk in their suffering to even notice.'

What is this place? Kate was about to ask, but as they stepped into the smoky light, she already knew the answer to her question. She had been here before with Louise on the Ghost Walk. The tunnels had led them to Cairncross Close. They were entering the Plague Quarter.

When they had entered before, with the Haunts Tour, the underground city had been empty, and had just held the scent of cold stone. Now the street was crowded with people. The stench clutched at the throat, making you want to retch and choke. Some of the houses at either side were boarded up; raw planks of wood covering the window spaces, the doors daubed with prayers and a red cross.

A cart moved slowly ahead of them. Limbs, some still limp and flopping, some stiff with rigor mortis, poked out from under a filthy length of cloth which had been roughly flung over to cover the cargo of death. A man rode on the side, hardly less skeletal and filthy than the corpses his feet were resting upon. As the cart rumbled on, he turned from time to time, scrawny neck straining, calling up to the houses either side for people to bring out their dead. A wretched throng swarmed all around the wagon; men carrying bundles, women carrying babies and children. The crowd moved blindly, heads down, stepping over bodies which lay slumped against walls or huddled in doorways. For these there was no help, they were dying where they fell.

No one tried to stop Jack and his crew, or interfere in any way, but they were moving against the flow of the crowd and progress was slow. The people were all going in the same direction and most were heavily burdened, with household goods, pots and pans dangling from their packs, some even had stools and chairs tied to their backs. The stream of people, the hopeless dogged looks on their faces, reminded Kate of the lines of refugees that she had seen on the TV news, leaving some godforsaken trouble spot. They were obviously fleeing from something, but what?

At the end of the street, all became clear. A wall had been built up to the level of the tops of the houses. It was new, thrown together, the mortar still wet and oozing.

People were grouped in front of the barrier. Some just stared, unbelieving. Others scrabbled at the base of it, their fingers torn and bleeding from trying to tear it down.

'But I am not sick!' one man called out, echoing the distress of those around him.

'Then you soon will be,' another laughed, showing black stumps where his teeth should be. He was a large man, big and brawny, and wore a soft hat pulled well down over his forehead. 'They have abandoned us to our fate. There's no point,' he said, to a boy trying to dig his way into the mortar. 'The watchmen have set guard on the other side. Even if we break out, they will kill us. What do you think, friend?' He was addressing Jack. 'What will you do? You and your lad here? You look healthy enough.'

He was talking about Govan. Kate looked at Tom and Elinor. The man did not see them. Neither did anybody else. She shivered. It gave her a funny feeling. Being a ghost.

'We are going to Carfax,' the man continued. 'We have heard there is another way out. We have heard they have yet to block that. Do you want to try it?'

Jack nodded, his chin deep in his scarf, but he gave no sign of moving. The two men gave them a strange look and the bigger one seemed ready to challenge Jack further, but his friend pulled him away, with a muttered, 'We will be too late!'

The two moved off after the crowd streaming away from the wall. The crew was just about to follow when shots rattled out. Kate's blood chilled, thinning to iced water, as a distant wailing cry hit the air. The shots rang out again and that one voice was joined by many others, a high keening scream of utter despair.

The crowd was turning, the road ahead churning with people. Govan led them away, dodging through houses and back along alleys, first this way, then that, but everywhere the same thing had happened. All routes in and out of this part of the city had been bricked up. Every avenue of escape was closed to them.

The shouts and cries intensified. The sound of the crowd was coming from all directions and getting closer. The tone had changed from miserable hopelessness to anger. Maddened beyond endurance by the terrible fate imposed upon them, the sad stream of individuals seeking escape was about to turn into a mob: a mindless raging monster which would rampage through the streets left to it, taking its fury out on anyone in its path.

Govan had lead them to Carfax, the ancient crossroads which quartered the town, leading to all the main parts of the city. Walls had been newly built across three of the thoroughfares. The road they were in was the only one open.

Kate, Elinor and Tom looked to Jack, thinking he would know what to do, but his face was greying with panic.

13

'There's no escape.' Jack looked about. 'The roads out are blocked. The houses on either side boarded up. We are caught like rats in a trap. That man was suspicious. If they come back and find us here they will certainly see us for strangers and tear us to pieces.' He drew his sword. 'Get behind me. I'll hold them off for as long as I can.' He gave his pistol to Kate. 'One shot is all you will have, so make it count.'

The distant cries and shouts of anger were getting nearer. Kate held the pistol tight and tried to keep it steady. The butt slipped and jumped in her hand as she crouched with the others behind a makeshift barricade, back against the wall. The shops and houses each side were boarded. The road they faced looked empty but the light of many torches already flickered up the sides of the farthest buildings . . .

'Perhaps you'd better let me have that,' Tom whispered in her ear.

'No way.' Kate held the pistol two-handed. 'Jack gave it to me.'

'Well, quit waving it about. You're likely to blow someone's head off.'

'I thought that was the whole idea.'

'Them. Not us.'

Jack turned with a gesture to keep quiet.

'Hang on.' Tom stepped forward.

'Tom!' Kate screamed at him. 'What are you doing! Get back – they'll see you!'

'Do as she says, boy,' Jack shouted. The mob were rounding the corner, headed by the large brawny man in the slouch hat. 'They are nearly upon us!'

'No,' Tom strolled calmly backwards and forwards. 'Don't you see? Haven't you noticed it?'

'See what? Kate asked. "Notice what?"

'The light – it's changing. Look around you.'

Govan and Jack thought the boy had gone mad. They gestured frantically for him to get back. Govan made a grab for Elinor, but his hand was becoming transparent, it had no more grip than a plastic glove. It fell like a leaf from her sleeve as she stepped forward to follow her brother. Kate saw that Tom was right. Somehow they had come back to their own time. The ghost crew were fading to mere outlines. Even the pistol in her hand had lost its substance. It dropped silently to the ground as she stood up slowly to join her cousins.

The red, rolling smoky darkness had gone, replaced by discreetly-hidden electric light. The smell had gone, too, and the ground beneath their feet was dry clay, not filthy sucking mud. Kate listened. There was no shouting angry mob. The only sound was of somebody talking. Kate knew the voice immediately.

'This place was called Carfax,' Louise was saying. 'It marks one of the ancient crossroads of the city and exactly mirrors the modern interchange above it. It has not long been discovered. Until recently it lay behind . . .'

As Kate joined Tom and Elinor the wall in front of them began to fade, the stone become transparent. They stepped easily through, back into their own time, and joined the group who were standing round listening to Louise.

'What about Davey?' Elinor whispered urgently. 'He's not here or anything . . .'

'Why should he be?' Tom answered.

'Well, where do you think he is? What do you think has happened to him? What if we can get out, but he can't? We can't just leave him! What if . . .'

'I don't know!' Kate whispered back fiercely. Elinor was echoing her own thoughts. Relief at their own escape was rapidly turning to fear for her brother. 'Ssh, a minute. I have to think . . .' she added, hoping to stop her cousin from worrying, although she had no idea what to do.

'Who's that?' Louise broke off what she was saying, craning her head, looking about to locate the whispering voices which were interrupting her talk.

'Where did you spring from?' she said, her tone turning from irritation to consternation. Muttered amazement spread through her audience until the whole group turned to stare at them as if they were ghosts. 'I thought you had left us.'

'We did,' Tom said. 'But we came back.'

'We've just been a little bit behind most of the way,' Kate added quickly. Their return had caused quite a stir and the guide's surprise was turning to suspicion.

'What about your brother – didn't you find him, then?' Louise was frowning, her eyes narrowing.

'Yes, but . . . Davey decided . . . decided to stay outside. Like somebody said, he's a little claustrophobic.'

'Should have thought of that before he came on the tour, shouldn't he?' Louise was still not happy. She couldn't quite say exactly what, but there was something odd going on here.

'He didn't know,' Kate shrugged. 'Now he does.'

'Well, you've rejoined us right at the end of this evening's tour.' She turned back to the group. 'We will now be taking a short cut, ladies and gentlemen, which will bring us out near our starting point.'

Louise trudged off. Even if Carfax wasn't strictly the end of the tour, it was now. She'd had enough. She was already tired and had more walks to do including the Eerie Pub Crawl and Midnight Graveyard Terror Tour. This lot had really taken it out of her. First those kids appearing and disappearing, and then the group had all got very jittery, particularly in the underground city. She leaned on her skull-headed staff, waiting for the stragglers to catch up. This was just a job and she could do without kids messing about – freaking people out. Personally, she didn't believe in any of this ghost stuff . . .

'Ahh!' one of the American women – the one with the cardigan – let out a yell.

Louise gave a sigh of irritation. What was it now?

Then more joined in. The Japanese girls were jumping around as if they had been jabbed by pins.

'What's up?' Louise asked, trying to sound as though she cared. 'What's the matter?'

'I – I thought I saw something . . . I definitely *felt* something . . .' the woman held her hands to her lips. Her face was pale ivory.

'And me,' one of the Japanese girls joined in.

'Me, too,' her friend said, pointing to her own chest.

'What? What did you see?' Louise demanded impatiently.

'A little boy,' the American woman said, 'about so high. Little white face and dark, dark eyes. He was looking straight at me . . .'

Louise looked up in alarm. Not that she was going to tell them, of course, but psychics had seen this boy before, usually in the street at the top of the steps playing a penny whistle.

The Japanese girls nodded vigorously.

'He has a man with him,' one said, her eyes wide. 'Long dark hair. Dressed in olden time clothes . . .'

Louise regarded her flock over the top of her staff's plastic skull. They were speaking in the present tense, for heaven's sake. It was definitely time to go. She could see nothing herself, but she thought she had

83

better get them topside before they all started completely wigging out.

'Our tour for this evening is drawing to a close follow me for the quickest route back to the surface thank you for using Haunts Tours ladies and gentlemen do join us again and I do hope you have enjoyed your evening.'

Louise rattled through the sign off section of the Haunts script at record speed, hoisted her long skirt to show sturdy Doc Marten boots and strode off, leading them as fast as she could, heading for the door by the side of the cathedral which would take them out of the underground city.

Kate exchanged looks with Tom and Elinor. The tourists had been describing Jack and Govan. The two ghosts had managed to escape, too, and they were staying with them, shadowing the group. Kate could see them as clearly as she could see the other people on the tour. She had almost laughed out loud at Govan's antics with the Japanese girls and gave him a little wave as he and Jack went on ahead. She was very glad that they were still around. While they were there she felt in touch with her brother. Where was he now? Any relief at returning to her own time was cancelled by the horror of leaving him behind. What would happen if all connection with the Ghost City suddenly snapped? What if he could not get back? Kate shuddered to think of leaving her brother in a place that no one even knew existed.

14

Davey trotted along the silent streets as quiet as his ghost companions. They were going back to the Market Square, following more or less the same route as the Ghost Walk. When they reached the square, they had to cross to the cathedral. That's where they would meet Jack, Govan and the others. Davey hoped that they were all right. He'd tried asking Polly what she thought might be happening to them, but she had brushed his questions aside. Maybe she was still annoyed about the tea shop. Whatever the reason was, she was saying very little.

Polly was not speaking because she did not want to frighten him. Davey seemed a brave enough boy, he was coping well with the strangeness of the Ghost City, but he was not in tune with its different moods and atmospheres, how could he be? Tonight was queer. Different from anything even in her long experience. Perhaps it was the Gathering. Gatherings happened all the time and they were of differing kinds. Light Gatherings were happy, joyous events, a chance for crews from the city and beyond to meet and mingle freely. Dark Gatherings were sombre occasions, when crews were brought together to witness some ritual ceremony of sacrifice and punishment. She felt none of the spring-like feeling which accompanied the former times, rather the opposite. She drew her cloak nearer to her. As they drew nearer the Market Square, she felt violence and hatred thickening around them, filling the air like a bloody mist. But she had promised the boy's sister. She had to get him there, one way or another.

'The streets are awfully empty,' Davey commented to Elizabeth. 'Where is everybody?'

'I don't know.' The thought had struck her, too. 'Gone to the Gathering, I expect.'

'What exactly are Gatherings?' Davey asked.

'Things that happen every now and then to entertain people, allow them to forget their feuds and get together. They draw interest from every crew in the city. They can be great fun. Unless . . .'

'Unless what?'

Elizabeth looked up, afraid that she had said too much. Polly indicated with a shake of her head not to speak further, but it was too late.

Davey had stopped in the middle of the street, fists curled, frowning ominously. He'd had enough of being kept in the dark about everything.

'I'm not going any further until you tell me.'

'It's a kind of a spectacle,' Polly explained reluctantly, urging him to hurry on. They were not far from Fiddler's Court, the Judge's House. He had picked one of the worst possible places to stop. 'An event from the history of the city is acted out . . .'

'What kind of event?' Davey held out stubbornly. 'I won't budge 'til I know, so don't push me.'

'It could be anything, but at a Dark Gathering it is likely to be something unpleasant. Battles, burnings, torture, floggings, accidents, murders, massacres, executions,' Elizabeth numbered them on her fingers, 'are relived in every agonising detail.'

'Do people enjoy seeing that?' Davey asked, his face registering horror as they walked on.

'Some undoubtedly do, that depends on the crew, but like it or not, they have no choice but to watch.'

'What do you mean?'

'They are summoned to witness the consequences of insubordination or disobedience.'

'Do you know who will be punished?'

'Not until the Judge opens the Book of Possibilities. It is all written there. What was, what is, and what is to be. Listen.' Elizabeth inclined her head in the direction of the square. A distant mutter came towards them. 'I think it has started already.'

'Hush, Elizabeth!' Polly hissed and looked round fearfully as they came to the last corner.

When she realised where they were, her anxiety became even more pronounced. She had thought to avoid Fiddler's Court and to approach the Square from a different direction, but now she found they were in the dread space, right in front of the Judge's House. How had that happened?

She glanced round fearfully, looking for Sentinels, but there was no sign of them. It was as though they had been withdrawn. They had not seen sight nor sound of them in goodness knows how long. Not once had they had to evade them. It was as if the Sentinels could not be bothered to hunt them, as if there was no need . . .

'*If your name is in the Book, there's no hinder and no help.*'

That was one of the sayings of the city. Ghosts were deeply fatalistic. It meant that the bullet had your name on it; that there was no escape, your fate was sealed. Polly's worry was deepening by the minute, developing into the profoundest alarm. If they were caught by the Judge there was no telling what would happen. The boy would be enslaved. His soul taken, he would be sent back into the world to do the Judge's evil bidding. As for herself and Elizabeth? They would be punished and then turned into wraiths, their spirits stripped away. What good is a ghost without a spirit? It did not bear thinking about.

'Ssh,' she breathed. 'No more talking. Quiet as cats now. We must move on.'

They were nearly there. The street they were in opened directly on to the Market Square. The big open space was full of people. At the centre of the crowd stood the Market Cross, tall and massive on its granite pedestal. Every head was turned in one direction. On the far side of the square, practically in front of the doors of the cathedral, stood a large wooden platform. A man was standing, arms folded, looking out at the crowd from behind a leather mask. The leaping fire and torchlight gleamed on his sweating torso. Like the crowd, he was waiting for something.

The square was set for a hanging. Polly turned, seeking a way back. She knew without being told who the gallows were for. She had seen it all before. They were walking straight into a trap.

15

They had not gone five metres when a motorbike roared into life. Davey turned to glimpse a tattered leather jacket, lank fair hair and the scarred pock-marked face of the Recent Dead above the flaring headlights.

'That's them.' Someone gunned another engine. 'Get 'em!'

Headlights lit the sides of the buildings. A whole bunch of them had left Market Square and were strung across the narrow street from one side to the other. Polly gathered Davey and Elizabeth to her and they fled, turning down one street, then another, in a wild bid to escape the snarling machines, but more bikes joined in the hunt, and still more. Headlights lit every junction, herding them, directing their fight.

They turned a final corner and found themselves back in Fiddler's Court. A ring of motorbikes purred forward, guiding their quarry into Blythe Lane. Polly looked round in desperate panic. Blythe Lane was a dead-end. The bikes ranged themselves across the entrance, cutting off any chance of escape. A side door opened, spilling light on to the cobbles.

The motorbikes came towards them at walking pace,

forcing them back to where a dark figure stood in the open doorway.

'We done what you said, sir.' The leader of the gang dipped his head in deference. 'We got 'em for you.'

The man he addressed was tall and wore all black. A white, curling wig hung down to his shoulders. A wide-brimmed, black hat shaded a face criss-crossed and spider-webbed with lines. His skin had the yellowed, wrinkled look of withered fruit. Small eyes nestled deep in sunken flesh under jutting eyebrows grey and snarled, like barbed wire. His expression was pitiless, indifferent. His eyes did not blink and they were hardly recognisable as human: dark enough to seem to have no pupils, as cold and hard as polished stones.

He nodded to the motorcycle crew standing in front of him.

'Bring them.'

'What about us?' the lank haired youth whined. 'You said . . .'

'You can have what's left.' The Judge's thin lips pulled back from yellow teeth as he stepped back from the doorway. 'Hurry now. Inside. I haven't much time.'

The Judge's room was long and gloomy, the corners lost in shadows. Fat guttering candles stood on iron stands at either end of a large carved oak table. It held a big black ledger flanked by skulls painted with strange devices. The Judge rested his hand on one of these, two long bony

91

fingers curling into the empty eye sockets. With the other hand he opened the book, letting the cover fall with a bang, sending up a cloud of dust. The vellum pages of the book were stiff and wrinkled like skin, they crackled as he turned them.

'Polly Martin, Jack Cade's paramour.' He found her name and looked up, staring across at her, fingers steepled. 'Your lover has ever been a thorn in my flesh. This time he has gone altogether too far and will have to be punished . . .'

'Where is he?' Polly demanded. 'What have you done with him?'

'Nothing. Yet.' A skull-like grin stretched the Judge's skin. 'But as I allowed you to see, the crowd awaits him.'

'What about Govan?' Elizabeth spoke up. 'And the others with him?'

'Elizabeth Hamilton.' He fixed her with his black-eyed stare. 'Ah, here you are, my dear.' He turned another page and his bony finger moved down the list of entries, stopping at her name. 'A relative newcomer. Not that I take that as any excuse.' He moved round from his side of the table and began to pace in front of them, a tall, gaunt, terrifying figure. 'You thought to defy me? Me?' He paused to allow the enormity of their crime to sink in. 'You know the rules. You must suffer the consequences. All breaches between this world and the other are to be reported immediately. Living inter-lopers are to be handed over. Immediately. Punishment for disobedience is swift and inevitable. And you know what that is?'

Polly and Elizabeth nodded.

'For the benefit of those who don't,' he turned now to Davey, 'anyone breaking this rule will suffer their own death. Over and over again.'

He seemed to like the idea of that. His hooded eyes found Polly. He smiled as her hand went to her breast.

'Now, Elizabeth. What was your death?' He turned to consult the ledger. 'Ah, yes. Trampled by a horse, and then run over by a carriage. Tell me,' he was smiling at her now. 'Did it hurt? Or did you feel nothing after the first blow?' He noted a flicker in her face. 'I see that was indeed the case.' His own expression took on a look of mock sympathy and he shook his head slowly. 'I fear that you will not be so lucky this time, my dear.'

'I do not care what you do.' Elizabeth's grey eyes stared steady defiance. 'I care nothing for you, or your Black Sentinels, or the disgusting mindless morgue sweepings you call a crew!'

'Enough! Hold your tongue!' He towered over her, his voice hissing with hatred. 'Your whole crew will suffer for what you have done. Jack will be hung. The brat Govan will go back to his former mistress, that in itself is punishment enough. As for you – I can make you suffer for all eternity!'

'That's not fair!' Davey stepped between them. 'Leave

her alone! It's not right to punish her. She was just trying to help us!'

'Right? Fair?' He laughed down at him. 'How little you know of the world in which you find yourself. It is no use snivelling now. You blundered in here, Davey Williams. You cannot expect others to guide you out.'

'How do you know my name?'

'I know everything – about you and your sister and your cousins.'

'Where are they?'

'That is not for you to know.' He smiled again. 'Suffice it to say that they will shortly be in *my* keeping. Along with the other members of this crew of fools.'

'What are you going to do to them?' Davey lunged towards him, but one look from the glittering eyes held him helpless.

'All in good time.' The Judge laughed again. 'Such courage in one so young. You begin to show promise.' He put a hand out towards Davey, his touch as cold as an icicle. 'You will do well.'

'What do you mean?'

'The living have value here. We find . . . uses . . . for them. But, as I said, all in good time . . . Bring them,' he ordered.

Black figures glided in from the shadowy corners of the room and seized them with a strength that made struggling pointless.

'Where are you taking us?' Polly wanted to know.

'You are to come with me, my dear,' the Judge said with his blood-freezing smile. 'We are to attend a hanging. I would not like you to miss it. After all, it is someone you know.'

16

Kate, Tom and Elinor kept close to Louise as she led the way out of the tunnel. If they stayed with her, stayed with the Haunts Tour, maybe they would get back to the real world and find that none of this had happened. It had all been some kind of dream, some kind of weird illusion. Maybe Davey had just left the tour an hour before and made his own way back to the Market Square. He would be waiting there for them.

The door opened into a stone-flagged basement area. Hope leapt in Kate's chest as she saw that the wrought-iron gate at the top was painted in black and gold. She had noticed that on the way to the Ghost Walk; the council was painting the railings all through the Old Town as part of their heritage refurbishment.

For a moment she thought that they were, indeed, back in their own time; but the sky above was dark, darker than it should have been. She stumbled and all her fear flooded back again, as the steps beneath her feet began to change; the surface of the stone becoming worn and broken, the corners cushioned with dark green moss. She slipped on a patch of a slime and went to grab railings that were no longer there. She would have fallen had Tom not caught her arm.

'What's happening?'

She looked at her cousins. Panic was filling their eyes, too.

'It's all changing back again.'

'Why?'

Tom shrugged, 'I don't know.'

They stood by, helpless, as the substantial figure of Louise, not to mention the others on the Haunts Tour, became less and less solid, fading to transparent outlines. It was like being trapped in some dreadful game; they were helpless to stop this happening again. There was absolutely nothing that they could do about it.

'. . . Knowlegate,' Louise was saying. Her voice was cutting in and out, as if she was talking under water or running on faulty batteries. '. . . beside the cathedral . . . gate means street . . . street by the burial mound . . . prehistoric site . . .'

They were standing by the side of the cathedral. It loomed above them, a solid mass of stone soaring up into a matt black sky. There were no lights in the great glass windows and no noticeboards outside showing the opening times and services. Kate felt the cold grip of fear tighten inside her. All evidence of Louise and her party had gone. She looked round. There was no sign of Govan, nor of Jack Cade. They were completely alone.

'Where is everybody?' Elinor's eyes were huge with fear. 'What's happening?'

'I – I don't know.' Tom held a finger to his lips. 'Ssh a minute, will you? Hear that?'

The other two nodded. There was a hushed ripple of excitement coming from the direction of the Market Square. As they listened, the rustling murmur of the crowd grew in strength, erupting into a deep throated roar.

'Something big is going on down there.' Tom bent his head in the direction of the noise. 'Sounds like the home team running on to the pitch.' He beckoned the others forward. 'I reckon we'd better take a look.'

They stayed close to the cathedral's stone walls, flitting like shadows from buttress to buttress, until they came to the end of Knowlegate.

Nothing prepared them for the horror waiting there. They shrank back, seeking the comforting shelter of stone, unable to even blink their eyes at sights hideous enough to paralyse. They leaned, backs against the wall, hardly able to breath at all, swallowing back the terror that filled their throats like the sickening taste of bitter bile.

Knowlegate opened directly on to Market Square. A vast crowd was gathered there; a sea of people stretching back and back. You could see at a glance that these were not human, not living. Collected here, dressed in costumes from every age, was every ghost crew in the city. Some were almost skeletons, robes over bones, faces in different stages of decay, the flesh eaten away. Some showed obvious evidence of what had brought them here: limbs hanging in shattered splinters, skulls cleaved with dark cavities. Others looked fresh, contemporary, as though they had just stepped out for an evening stroll. Except for their faces: holes for eyes and ghastly white skin, leprous, shiny, almost fluorescent.

All were turned upwards, all were turned one way.

The children were turning in the same direction, trying to find the focus of the crowd's attention, when a familiar figure darted out of the edge of the crowd. He was clearly very upset, black eyes huge in his head. His mouth worked in his little chalk-white face, trying desperately to form words. He grabbed Kate's arm, pointing towards the focus of the crowd.

'Nnnk! Nnnk!'

Govan pulled them into the porch of the cathedral. An ancient place of sanctuary; a place to see and not be seen. Almost in front of them stood a gallows. A huge wooden structure, newly-built, Kate could smell the raw wood. A hangman, leather-masked and jerkined, body oiled with sweat, stretched and tested the noose.

Kate understood now what Govan was trying to say: 'Jack, Jack.' The highwayman stood, legs chained at the ankle, hands manacled behind his back. The hangman moved to fit a hood over Jack's head. He shrugged it away, and continued to stare out at the crowd, defiant to the last.

Kate watched, horror mounting afresh inside her, as the hangman took him backwards, positioning him over the trap door. He reached up for the noose, testing the knot again, pulling it down, fitting it over Jack's head until the heavy rope rested on his shoulders. He gave the knot one more tug, tightening it slightly, and then he stepped back, ready to operate the lever which worked the trap door mechanism.

Govan stood, eyes wide, hands stuffed in his mouth. Kate put her hand on his bony shoulder, seeking to comfort him; his whole body was rigid, shaking with terror and fear. Everything seemed to be happening in slow motion. It was as if they were all caught, frozen in some sort of ritual. Tom had his mouth open, as if to say something, but no sound was coming out.

'Over there,' he managed to gasp at last. 'Not on the platform! At the base of the steps leading up to it!'

He pointed to a small group huddled close, guarded by tall black-robed figures. Polly, Elizabeth and Davey stood together; each of them bound like Jack, arms tied behind their backs.

What was held in store for them? Tom looked back at the platform and his eyes grew wide with terror. Other instruments of execution stood ready: muskets propped in a wigwam, next to crushing implements like huge wheels. A tall man dressed all in black was mounting the scaffold, long white locks framed a face shaded by a wide-brimmed hat. He had a massive book tucked under one arm. At the corner of the platform stood a lectern. As he set the tome down the crowd grew quiet, a hush of expectation spreading back from the front most ranks.

'What are we going to do?' Tom asked, his voice shaking.

'I – I don't know.'

Kate felt herself crack. She was the eldest. The others were looking to her. Even Govan's dark eyes were upon her, his small cold fingers gripping hers. She closed her own eyes, shutting out their panic-stricken faces. Tears squeezed from between the lids and she put a hand to her mouth to stifle a sob of despair.

17

Resistance was useless. Davey had long ceased struggling. By his side Polly stood resigned and Elizabeth held herself perfectly calm. Davey wanted to be like them, but it was a struggle not to cry. His wrists hurt where they were tied and tears welled up inside. He wished he had never suggested the Ghost Walk; if only the others had listened when he'd changed his mind about it. He wondered where they were now. Had they got away? It was very lonely and frightening being here on his own. Would he ever see them, his own time, his own home again? Davey did not have a clue what was going to happen to him, not the faintest idea; but the thing that made his eyes fill and the tears finally spill down his cheeks in salty streams, was that nobody would ever know.

There was no hope for him, but what about the others? Jack was going to be hung, but what about Govan? He wasn't here with them. What had happened to him? Davey remembered something about a blind man. The Blind Fiddler, that was it. The Blind Fiddler was the one who could get them all out of here. Weren't they supposed to meet him?

Davey turned to Elizabeth, nudging her with his shoulder.

'The Blind Fiddler,' he whispered.

'What about him?'

'Weren't we supposed to meet him?'

'Yes,' the girl whispered back. 'But only Govan can summon him and do you see him here?'

A Black Sentinel turned, silencing them with his empty skull gaze. The execution was about to commence. The Judge was mounting the steps, ready to pronounce sentence.

'How does he do it?'

'How does he do what?'

'Summon the Blind Fiddler. How does he do it?'

'With his pipe. He knows a special tune. The Blind Fiddler will always come. He is very fond of Govan . . .'

Bony fingers bit into their shoulders commanding silence. Above them, the Judge's voice rang out, as cold and harsh as metal on stone. Davey forced his mind away from it, blocking out the list of accusations. He shut his eyes and took himself back to his first moments in this strange, terrifying world, until he was standing on the steps, and the sound of a pipe was summoning him and the whole world was starting to shimmer . . .

Davey had always known he was a little bit different. There were his feelings about things, his premonitions. The way he sometimes knew what was going to happen before it happened. There was only a small gap between that and what he was trying to do now. If you think hard enough, try hard enough – that's what his gran said – anything was possible. Davey had tried before, just in small ways, sometimes it worked, sometimes it didn't. Now he concentrated everything, every ounce of his being, on that one moment, on hearing that high plaintive note again, on keeping it clear in his head.

A single note sounded in answer to his call, cutting through the air. Higher and higher it went, to a point where it seemed to be joined by another instrument, a violin. The two fused and blended, taking the sound well beyond the bounds of human hearing.

The music was so beautiful it made him ache inside. Davey opened his eyes to look around and could not believe his eyes. Next to him the Black Sentinels were caging their ears with skeletal fingers, writhing in silent agony. One by one they began to disappear . . .

Polly and Elizabeth were not affected at all, but the music seemed to be dissolving everything and everybody else: the platform, the gallows, the muskets, instruments of torture, the crowd itself, all were becoming transparent. The Judge alone seemed unchanged. Then he too began to fade, his dark form falling like black snow. Jack stepped out of his chains and walked past him without a second glance.

Davey's hands were free. He looked across the emptying square to see Govan, eyes closed, standing on the cathedral steps, pipe to his mouth, fingers flying over the stops, his music weaving spells strong enough to dismiss the ghosts and call up other forces. Kate, Elinor and Tom were by his side caught in the power of his playing. Finally, when all of the ghosts had gone, he stopped.

'Davey! Davey!' Kate called across the square, shouting her brother's name into the vibrating silence.

They ran towards each other, meeting in the middle of the square, hugging, not knowing whether to laugh or cry, while around them the world changed and changed again. All that mattered was that they were together again.

They did not know it, but the Ghost World was not in one stable time and place, it existed on different planes, in different dimensions, one layered on top of another.

Jack and the rest of his crew stood back grave-faced, looking about them in worried silence. They knew. They did not share in the children's relief and had no idea what would happen next. The plane of the ghost crews was evaporating, that was true, but to be replaced by what? Even as they watched, a rising fog came from nowhere, rolling along the ground, creeping to fill the Market Square, rising up to cover everything, the Market Cross, the buildings. Even the huge solid bulk of the cathedral was beginning to fade, to be rendered insubstantial.

The mist began to part and, for a second, there was a gleam of light, a snatch of music before the greyness surged back. A figure was coming towards them: tall, black-hatted, with a dark cloak wrapped around him.

He stood for a moment, as though tasting the air, and then came forward. His broad-brimmed hat shaded a face so similar to the Judge's that they could have been brothers. Except that this man's face was open and kind, his mouth wide and generous. Blind eyes showed blue-white, bulging like marbles. Under his cloak, as if cradling something very precious, he held a violin.

'Who summons me here?' he demanded, his low voice sounding like a deep bell. 'Who calls up such powerful magic?'

Govan stepped towards him and took his hand. The long tapering fingers traced the contours of the boy's face.

'Govan? What do you do, child? In this place? On this night? When you know the risk you take . . .'

Suddenly he looked up, as if aware that they were not alone.

'For your friends?' His head turned to take them in. 'You would do this for your friends?' His hand groped about, taking first Jack's hand, then Polly's. 'Jack Cade and his crew. And who are these others?' His hand brushed over Kate, Tom and Elinor, lighting on Davey's shoulder. 'Is this the one?'

Govan nodded.

His fingers moved over Davey's features with a touch as delicate as butterfly wings. He had heard tell of this boy.

Somehow his life was linked with the life of the city, but in what ways, and how, and to what end, it was even beyond the Fiddler's powers to understand.

'Do not blame yourself, child.' The blind eyes rolled down towards Davey, the man's face creased in a smile. Davey looked up in wonder, it was as if the old man was reading his face and mind at the same time. 'You did not mean to lead yourself or your kin into danger. Tell me,' his voice was soft and gentle. 'How did you find your way in here?'

'I – I leaned on a mirror,' Davey stammered, 'and, and I was through. It was like going through a door.'

'Where was this mirror?'

'In a special little room. In the underground city.'

'How was the room shaped? Was it shaped differently?'

'Yes, it was,' Davey replied. 'It had about eight sides, and it had strange stuff in it.'

The blind man nodded as if Davey was confirming something he knew already.

'It was a place ever used for magic,' he said. 'And not of the best kind. It sounds as if some new group have taken it now and are meddling in things they have not the wit or knowledge to control or understand.'

'Blind Fiddler,' Jack stepped forward, taking again his position as spokesman and leader of the crew. 'Can you open a way to get them back? They have suffered already and have earned the Judge's enmity. We must get them away from here – and soon.'

107

'I will do my best, but it will not be easy. The ways are closed from this part of the city.' He turned around, his blind eyes searched the misty darkness and then returned to a fixed point, as though obeying some kind of internal compass. 'The City is criss-crossed with lines, invisible to the eye, but I can feel them moving through me. They carry the earth's energy. Strange things can happen at points where they cross each other. One world can open into another.'

'Are there many of these places?' Davey asked.

'Not many and they do not open readily. There is a powerful line running through Cannongate and across the river. The gate and bridge direct the flow of energy, they act like a channel focusing on one point. If we can get to this point at the right time . . .'

'Come then. Let us find the place.' Jack was uneasy. There was strangeness abroad. He did not like this mist curling round them, it smacked of magic and enchantment. He shivered, the atmosphere was eldritch enough to chill a ghost's blood. The sooner the children were out of the city, the better. 'We must away.' He wrapped his long arms around himself. 'We must be close by the place of the Old Grey Man and his daughter. I feel the presence of the Unseelie Court.'

'This Old Grey Man,' Davey asked. 'Who is he?'

'King of the Unseelie Court. He leads the Host,' the Fiddler replied. 'They are the stuff of legend and story. They were here long before us, when all this was forest.

They have no love of humankind, dead or alive. They delight in making mischief and wreak havoc where they can.'

'And his daughter?'

His face twisted. 'She is the worst of them. She is very beautiful and very cruel. She has a weakness for human children. She takes them and keeps them—'

'Like changelings, you mean?' Kate frowned.

'They have been called that. Yes.'

'So – this Host – they are fairies?'

The Fiddler nodded. 'That is one of the names by which they are known. But these are not the harmless winged creatures of children's stories. The Host are human size with silver hair and silver eyes, but are ill disposed towards our kind.'

'But they don't still take children, surely?'

'I assure you that they do, my dear. The daughter took a boy this very evening, from the town across the river. He was with her. I heard him crying.'

Davey felt that funny feeling again, like centipedes creeping all over him. Silver hair and eyes . . . He had seen someone like that. Felt the chill of her gaze cutting into him, seeping deep inside, right through to his bones.

'I know who she's taken,' he said. 'I saw it! If only I'd done something . . . I could have stopped her.' He looked up at the Blind Fiddler, took his hand, beseeching. 'We can't leave him here!'

'There's no help you can give.' The blind man shook

his head. 'Nothing you can do. And we must away from this place. We have delayed too long already. Tonight is Midsummer Eve.' He cocked his head on one side, as though listening to some distant sound. 'Their revels are over. The Fairy Raid is about to start. The Host ride out.'

18

From somewhere near came the sound of unearthly music. Fiddles, pipes and harps combined in exotic, almost hypnotic harmonies, mixed with eerie laughter and wild high cries. Knowe is another word for knoll, Kate remembered, a grassy mound. Knowlegate ran by the side of the cathedral. The thinning mist revealed that the huge stone building had disappeared, melted away, to be replaced by a vague hump in the landscape, a low hill, a grassy mound.

The music seemed to spin through the air, weaving webs round them. As they watched, the dome opened, and light spilled from it, sending a broad finger of silver out into the night. Then the music and laughter stopped, replaced by the faint chink of bridles, the ring of many small bells.

'We must flee!' Jack cried, looking for the best route of escape.

'There is no time for that.' The Blind Fiddler's voice was fierce with urgency. 'They will see us! We must hide!'

But where? The night was dark, but the mist was clearing to reveal an open landscape with no cover, no trees, no buildings.

'By the cross.'

An ancient stone stood where the Market Cross had been, marking the meeting place of four raised causeways.

'Down by the side of it. In the ditch.'

The soft clash of unshod hooves and the jingle of bridles grew louder. Govan led the Fiddler as they all made for the refuge, flattening themselves against coarse grass and rough earth in their makeshift hiding place. Davey felt the old man's cloak go over him, heard his voice in his ear.

'They are almost upon us. Do not stir. No matter what happens, no matter what you see, lie still as a mouse under the hawk's eye. Remember, it is dangerous beyond measure to even look.'

Despite the words spoken, Davey watched, he couldn't help himself. One glimpse showed beings very different from the tiny winged creatures of fairy-tale and birthday card. These were as tall as humans, slender, clad in grey, with slanting silver eyes, foxy grins and sharp, white teeth. Some rode on milk-white ponies, others walked or marched, carrying finely-wrought silver lances, and leaf-shaped swords. As they passed, a forest of ghostly trees – grey and green – grew up all around them.

Davey stared, mesmerised. They wove their own world as they rode. The spectacular cavalcade went on and on. Accompanying the parade were trooping fairies of every shape and kind, some uncannily handsome, others grotesque. At the centre came an old man, grey-robed, grey-haired, grey-bearded. The Old Grey Man riding a tall, grey steed, caparisoned in lace as fine as cobwebs.

Behind him, on a dazzling white horse, silver bridle trailing silk, came another rider. She rode with light glowing all around her like a soft halo. She looked very young, very beautiful, lounging back in her silver saddle, with silver-blonde hair, silver-grey eyes. She was smiling, her eyes slanting and her mouth widened into a shark's grin. She was clad in cloth of pale gold, her gown so bright it seemed to dazzle and hurt the eyes.

Davey could hardly breathe. He was looking at a princess. The Old Grey Man's daughter. Queen of the place. Malevolence and power spread out from her like an icy aura. Davey could not tear his gaze away. His body tingled at the spectacle. His throat ached with desire. Part of him watched, appalled, repelled by what he was witnessing; but another part of him was so entranced by the cold beauty and magic that he would have crawled over broken glass to join the Fairy Raid.

Her long gown was parted at the front and fell draping down the sides of her steed. Davey glimpsed a small figure half hidden by the shimmering folds. A child was seated in front of her. She held him by the shoulders, her tapering fingers with their long silver nails gripping into his red coat. This was no fairy child. This was a human boy. His clothes, blue trousers, brown boots, vibrant scarlet jacket were the only strong colours in all the pale parade. Davey glimpsed a face, tear-streaked, confused, frightened, and knew who he was. It was the boy by the traffic lights, the one that he had seen before the Ghost Walk had even started. He should have saved him then. He would have gone to him now if strong hands had not pulled him back. For an old man, the Blind Fiddler was surprisingly strong.

'There is nothing you can do for him. Nothing!' he hissed in Davey's ear. 'She is far too powerful. She will turn your eyes to wood and your heart to stone.'

He held Davey face down, his hand over the boy's mouth, until the silvery jingle jangle of harness and bridle bells faded and the troop had wound its way down a woodland ride of its own making and was completely out of sight.

'That little boy,' Davey asked as soon as it was safe to speak. 'What will happen to him?'

'He will be kept, indulged and petted, a plaything for the Old Grey Man's daughter. But, at the end of seven years, they pay a taen,' the Blind Fiddler searched for the right word, one that he would understand. 'A tithe, a sacrifice.'

'Is there nothing we can do?'

'Not at the moment. Her will is not always accomplished, however. Look at Govan here.' He put his arm round the boy. 'He was such a one. Taken as a small child.' The Blind Fiddler's hand tightened on the boy's shoulder. 'Just like the one you saw there now. I saved Govan. Gave him to Jack for safe-keeping.'

The Blind Fiddler's words were heavy with unspoken accusation. His blind eyes rolled towards the highwayman walking by his side, but Jack said nothing, just bowed his head. They had moved from the Cross, taking the causewayed road which would one day be Fore Street, one of the finest streets in the city, a wide paved thoroughfare with grand fine buildings on either side, but now it was rutted and muddy, not much wider than a cart track.

'How come they haven't tried to get him back?'

'Govan did not get away undamaged.' The Blind Fiddler squeezed the boy's shoulder. 'The Old Grey Man's daughter dislikes imperfection. He is safe from her now.'

'What about that other little boy?' Davey could not get him out of his mind. 'Can't you help him?'

'There might be a way . . .'

'How?' Davey demanded. 'Tell me how!'

'Wait. Be patient.' The blind man put his hand up. 'There is more than one way to skin a cat.'

19

'There is something amiss.' Jack stopped at a point near the top of the gradually rising ground. The fog had nearly gone now and up ahead a strange light stained the sky. The dark clouds had an orange underglow as if there was a great city beyond. Even the air had changed. It was no longer neutral, it smelt different: a Twentieth Century mix of smoky fumes and petrol.

'I know what it is,' Tom said, excited by these signs of his own time. 'It's the lights of the city. There's this stuff they put in the lamps, see,' he explained to Jack. 'It's a type of gas called neon, and that's what's making the colour. What happens is—'

'I wouldn't be so sure,' Kate said, cutting short the science lesson.

The glow they could see was not a gentle orange neon. As they approached the crest of the low rise, an angry red boiled up and spread out, reflected off the base of the low hanging clouds.

The Blind Fiddler sniffed the air, his fine nostrils flaring, taking in the smell of smoke and burning.

They reached the top of the slope and looked down into an inferno. Fires were raging either side of the river. Flames bloomed everywhere, consuming wharves and warehouses, leaving them gutted. Buildings stood for a moment, etched skeleton black against the liquid crimson water, before falling, collapsing in upon themselves and each other. Plumes of flame and smoke leapt hundreds of feet into a night sky, split and bisected by moving fingers of light. Overhead, plane engines droned. A series of explosions shook the ground beneath their feet. The times had again changed. Downstream from the bridge the fires raged; the city was in the grip of one of the worst air raids in its history.

The bridge itself seemed to act as some kind of border. Perhaps, as the Blind Fiddler said, it carried some great line of power. Despite the mass destruction, it seemed un-affected and upstream from it the city lay in darkness, part of a different timescape.

Jack led them down to Cannongate. The gate led to the bridge and the two together directed the flow of the earth's energy, channelling it towards a focusing point on the other side of the river.

The bridge in front of them, the one they must cross on, was not the one that Davey had known all his life. This was stonebuilt with massive supports and it was narrow. Narrow enough to have crossing places zigzagged into the parapet; narrow enough for the road to lead straight through Cannongate, instead of being diverted around it. It was completely different from the new bridge, a wide elegantly soaring span of concrete. It would never have been able to take modern traffic. It would have

20

Tom heard Davey's shout and saw the danger they were in. He darted forward, dragging Kate and Elinor back. The enemy planes were getting nearer, the air was humming with the sound of their engines.

'There is more than one way to cross.' Polly pointed to the flight of steps which went down by the side of Cannongate to the river. A wide quay led upstream to where boats bobbed in the dark water. 'Before he took *The Seven Dials*, my father was a river man. He used to take me out with him when I was little. I practically grew up on it.'

'Polly, you are a genius!' Jack kissed her on the forehead. 'All of you, follow me.'

Jack was glad to be in charge again and he would make a better job of it this time. So far his leadership had only taken them into danger. He had failed his own crew, not to mention these children who had put their faith in him. What kind of man was he? His shame at his earlier captivity was doubled by being rescued by two boys, one of them dumb, and a blind old man. He had been duped by the Judge's trickery and was powerless in the face of the Unseelie Court, but he did know about boats. He would get these children back where they belonged if it was the last thing he did.

Moored to a distant quayside, he found a boat big enough to take all of them. 'Here! Over here!' He beckoned from a small wooden jetty. He did not want to shout too loud. Although there did not seem to be anyone about, in this world appearances are not to be trusted and he was not about to take any risks.

By the time they joined him, Jack had already scrambled down to a large rowing boat. Davey untied the rope and Jack rowed round to wide stone steps. He sculled well and seemed perfectly at home on the water. Davey wondered if he had once been a pirate as well as a highwayman.

'There is no need for you all to come with us.' Kate did not want the ghost crew to take any more risks on their behalf. 'We will be all right from here.'

'Is that so, Mistress Kate.' Jack shipped the oars and looked up at her. 'You know the river, do you? You can scull and steer through its currents and tides, the three of you? And, when − if − you get to the other side, you know where to go? You know the point of power better than the Fiddler here? Not only that, but you can save that child, the little boy?' The boat rocked as he stood up to step out of it. 'I wish you luck. Goodbye.'

'No, no.' Tom stepped in front of him. 'She didn't mean it like that. We still need you. What's the matter with you?' he hissed at his cousin.

'Nothing. I meant it for the best . . .'

'Well, do us all a favour in future, shut up, will you?

Here give me a hand, hold the prow. No, not there, the sharp end. That's better.'

Jack kept the craft steady while Tom and Kate held the prow to allow Govan to settle the Blind Fiddler up near the front. The boat had four oars. Jack took the front two, Tom and Kate the next, while Polly worked the rudder.

Davey sat right in the prow with Elinor. The bridge did seem to mark some kind of border. On the other side raged a fire storm of destruction while on this side all was quiet and tranquil. The bridge had not been hit. Yet. But in the sky above them the sound of the bombing planes had changed from a distant drone to a rumbling roar.

Suddenly, Davey saw them. They had changed their angle of approach and were coming in low, defying the anti-aircraft guns. They were intent on cutting the connection from one side of the city to the other. Using the river as a guide path, they were specifically targeting the bridge.

Davey twisted in his seat. The boat was being carried swiftly downstream but they did not seem to be getting any closer to the opposite shore. The river seemed to have stretched to a mile wide. With no motor, the boat seemed to crawl over the surface like a crippled bug. The combined force of current and tide was acting against them. The rowers' efforts were too weak, too puny to make any impression. They were being sucked nearer and nearer to the bridge.

The planes were above them. Davey saw the bays open,

the sticks of bombs falling, tumbling over and over towards the water. He shut his eyes tight and instinctively scrunched right down, even though the side of the boat would be no protection.

He covered his ears against a series of deafening explosions which never came. When he opened his eyes again, the planes were pulling up and away. The river was a new mass of flame. The massive bridge supports bulged outwards like a bent-kneed elephant. Huge chunks of the parapet had been torn away. Bigger and bigger pieces were tumbling down towards the water as the whole structure began to collapse.

In the prow of the boat, Davey and Elinor braced themselves. The rushing swell would hit them first. Numbed by what he saw, Jack let go of the oars. Kate and Tom sat motionless, frozen by what was about to happen. The boat began to spin and turn as the rudder lay slack in Polly's hands. Only Govan and his master seemed unaffected. The boy gazed at the old man, while the Blind Fiddler stared straight ahead. He seemed undisturbed by the destruction he could sense, but not see. A giant wave was heading in their direction. A wave that, in a matter of seconds, would swamp the small craft and destroy them all.

21

'What do you see child? What do you see?' The Blind Fiddler leaned forward, gripping his shoulder, whispering into his ear.

Davey lifted his head. He hardly dared look. The bridge was destroyed. A small part of the span extended out over the river, but it was leading nowhere. The stone supports which had carried it across to the other side stuck up from the water like stubby, broken teeth.

The strange thing was, though, the odd thing was . . .

'What?' the Blind Fiddler asked urgently. 'What is this strange odd thing?'

'This side. The side towards us, I mean, the river's gone calm. The big wave that was coming seems all spread out. And—'

'And what?'

'It's hard to describe,' Davey rubbed his eyes. Not sure whether he was imagining things. 'Do you see it, Ellie?'

'See what?'

'Connecting the two sides. It's like a bridge of light streaming across, solid but not solid, like a laser or something . . .'

Elinor just nodded, at a loss to describe exactly what she saw. The light seemed white, but there were colours in it, flashing iridescent. It appeared to be constant, but she sensed movement so fast it appeared to be still. And then she couldn't look any longer.

'It's getting too bright. It's hurting my eyes . . .'

The line of power extended right across the river. In one direction it led through Cannongate, up Fore Street, down the nave of the cathedral, out through the West Door, over the Market Square to the Cross and on, touching other ancient places of power, right across the country.

In the other direction, the bridge of light led over the river like a fusion of rainbows. As Davey watched it seemed to change: widening, flattening, growing more solid. There seemed to be people walking on the misty brightness. The sky above showed blue, not black, in the reflecting water. The rainbow bridge ended on the far shore at a point where Davey could see traffic lights winking red and green at a place where four roads met. He could see the new clock tower. The hands were nearing twenty past seven . . .

The boat was moving swifter now, Jack was pulling towards the shore with all his strength. Kate was tiring, Davey leapt to take her place. Time was of the essence. He must be there, be at that place.

22

Davey was on his feet before the boat touched the bank. He leapt the space and ran across the concrete quay and up the wide sweep of steps that led to the top of the bridge. The people he met were real, solid. He pushed through them to where crossing lights flashed: red, green, red again. He hardly stopped, dodging through traffic, running against the flow of pedestrians. He had to get to the other side of the road and he had to do it while he still remembered why.

'Hey, steady!'

The child came hurtling out of the crowd again, just like the first time, looking over his shoulder, rushing towards him. Davey put out a hand to slow him down. Same ladybird-red top, blue trousers, blue-grey terrified eyes.

'Are you OK?'

The child shook his head slowly, just – as he had done before.

'Have you lost your mum, your dad?' Davey dropped down to be on the same level as him.

The boy nodded slowly as the lights blinked back to STOP.

'We'd better go and find her then, hadn't we?'

The words came out strangely, slow and distorted. It was as if he had departed from a pre-rehearsed script, as if he wasn't supposed to be saying this. His mouth felt frozen, as if by dental anaesthetic. He fought the feeling of paralysis off, resisting the almost overwhelming temptation to let the boy go.

'Look,' he went on, 'there's a policeman over there.' His arm weighed heavy, he had trouble raising it to the level of his shoulder to point to the crossroads. 'Let's go and ask him, shall we?'

As Davey took the child by the hand, he glimpsed a face in the crowd. A woman was coming towards them, her hand outstretched to claim the child. She was beautiful, but very pale, her mouth a red-lipsticked slash, her face framed by pale blonde hair. For a second, their eyes met. Hers seemed to flash silver and he felt himself freeze, his insides turning into something heavy, as if he had swallowed a stone.

Nevertheless, Davey held tight to the child and carried on walking, even though his legs felt like rubber.

'Excuse me . . .'

As he approached the policeman, the woman retreated, her lips curled back in a snarl of absolute hatred. Her eyes glittered with fury, the look of an animal robbed of its prey, then she swerved away.

'Can I help you, son?'

'Yes. It's this little boy,' Davey began to say, 'I think he's, I think he might be—'

'Sam! Sammy!'

A middle-aged woman was running towards them, long grey-brown hair flying, her face distorted with grief and fear.

'Thank God! Oh, thank God!'

She gathered the child up into her arms and hugged him to her. The boy wrapped himself around her, bursting into tears, sobbing with relief. She held him fiercely, burying her face into the soft jersey material of his red jacket, before turning to the policeman.

'I don't know how to thank you, officer,' she said, wiping the tears from her face, 'I really thought . . .'

'It wasn't me, Madam. It was this young lad here. He—'

The policeman looked around but Davey had gone.

'Davey? Are you all right?' Kate's voice sounded muffled and far away. He looked up at her, his vision blurred, as though he was seeing through water.

'Yes. I guess.' His speech was croaky and thick, as if he had been asleep. His head felt muzzy, empty, like someone had wiped his circuits.

'I thought you were right behind me. I had to come back. And I find you rooted to the spot, staring into space like . . .' Kate broke off. 'Are you sure you're all right? You look a fit funny.'

'I'm fine.' Davey tried to put on a reassuring smile.

'There was something . . .' He looked round, suddenly

127

remembering the woman and the little boy. 'Did you see them?'

'See who?' Kate grabbed his hand, yanking him across the road. 'Come on, Davey. What's the matter with you?'

Kate had hold of his arm again and was pulling him along the pavement by his coat sleeve. Davey was just about to protest; he hated it when she did this. He was going to break away from her when he stopped. He looked at the people around them, wandering tourists, strolling families, and had that odd feeling: like this had happened before . . .

'This Ghost Walk thing was your idea . . .' Kate was saying. 'If you don't hurry we'll miss the start and it won't be worth going. Tom and El are waiting . . .'

'I don't want to go.' Davey thrust his hands in his pockets, his face set and sulky.

'What do you mean, you don't want to go?' Kate demanded. 'What do you want to do, then?'

'Spend the money in Pizza Hut. I told you before.'

'Not that again.' Kate rolled her eyes. Davey could be such a pain sometimes, especially when he went all stubborn on her. 'What do you two think?'

The twins had come over to see what was causing the delay. Kate turned to them now for support, expecting them to back her up.

Tom shrugged and looked at Elinor.

'Well, I . . .'

'For goodness' sake!' Kate yelled in exasperation. 'You're as bad as him! Why can't any of you stick to anything?'

Elinor looked away from Kate. All this shouting was attracting quite a crowd. One family in particular was really focusing in. An old man with a white stick had his head turned in their direction. He was with his son, or maybe it was his grandson; a handsome man, quite young, hawk-like features and long curling dark hair tied back in a pony tail. Even though it was midsummer, he wore a scarf round his neck, one of those with tassels, kind of like a prayer shawl. The woman with him, his wife probably, wore her dark hair tucked under a red kerchief. She was pretty with a clear-featured face and sharp black eyes which were looking over at them now, amused by their arguing. There was a girl about Kate's age, with long wavy brown hair, and a young lad, perhaps Davey's age, perhaps a bit younger . . .

Elinor frowned. She was certain she had never seen any of them before, but something about them seemed familiar . . .

The boy's dark eyes held hers for an instant, and then he gave a smile and a half-wave as the family began to make their way over the bridge. The couple held hands, the girl walked with them, looking down at the river. The boy kept company with the old man. The man's hand rested on the boy's shoulder, his stick tap-tapping against the metal rails of the bridge. For no reason at all this made her shiver.

'I'm with Davey on this,' she said, her voice decided and firm. 'Let's forget the Ghost Walk. We can always go some other time. I vote we have a pizza.'

Hallowe'ev

1

ALL HALLOWS EVE – ALL SOULS – SAMHAIN

Davey Williams copied the words carefully from the board.

—these are all names for the festival we call HALLOWE'EN.
HOMEWORK:
1) Write about the festival, its origins and customs around the world (see sheet from today's lesson).
2) Write about what (if anything) you did to celebrate.

One of Mr Craddock's more imaginative assignments, Davey thought as he finished writing and put his notebook away. He did not bother to copy the message scrawled across the bottom of the board: *ALL pumpkins MUST be finished BEFORE home time!!!* but he redoubled his efforts with his craft knife. There was only half an hour to go and he did not want to stay behind. Too much to do, what with trick or treating and the twins coming for half term.

You couldn't do anything without having to write about it: Christmas, Easter, every holiday period was the same. Davey was seriously tempted to put 'Nothing. Watched Television' in answer to Task 2, even though it wouldn't be true. Trouble was Craddock would know. He was organising the Hallowe'en Disco. Davey did not want to upset him. Mr Craddock was not exactly good-tempered, even at the best of times, and at the moment he was particularly frazzled. Davey could hear him shouting at people in the hall. Not that you could blame him. He was having to look after two classes. Davey's teacher was off sick, not likely to return until after Christmas, and the replacement wasn't starting until next half term.

Craddock would be back in a minute, stressing about the pumpkins. He wanted the best of them on display. Not that Davey's would come into that category. He couldn't get the teeth right. They would not go pointy, no matter how hard he tried. They were all stumpy. The more he whittled away at them, the worse they got. They were looking pretty gummy, to be honest, like a pump-kin-headed old man. Plus the eyes weren't right. One round, one square, they were uneven, lopsided, one bigger than the other.

'Self portrait?' A voice above him asked.

He looked up to see Lisa Wilson standing beside him. She was slim, small, wearing regulation dark blue sweat shirt over less than regulation jeans and trainers. Her unruly dark curls fluffed out round her triangular face and, as she grinned down at him, her wide apart grey eyes sparkled with amusement.

'Looks like the village idiot. You'll never scare the ghosts away with that thing.'

'Give it a rest, Lise,' Davey groaned. 'Craddock's already had a go at me about it.'

'Here let me have a go.'

She took the knife from him. 'Slice off this lot, for a start.' She removed the top set of stumps. 'Deepen these cuts here, widen the mouth . . .'

'Hey, that's really good.' Davey smiled up at her. 'Ever thought about being a dentist?'

'Nah, that'd be boring. I'm going to be an artist.'

She attacked the eyes and the nose and, in a few deft strokes, Davey's pumpkin was transformed. A wide, jagged mouth grinned wickedly beneath slanting eyes and a squat triangular nose.

'There. That's better.' Lisa was boring holes for the string now. 'We'd better take it along to the hall.'

Mr Craddock and most of the others were there already. Davey could hear him barking out orders halfway down the corridor. The rest of the class were putting up decorations and hanging banners for the disco. Craddock's temper was not improving. A series of small detonations set him off shouting at the boys blowing up black and orange balloons. Then the clunk and scrape of furniture across the floor sent him over to yell at another group lugging tables through the door.

'Don't drag them! You'll mark the parquet. Lift and carry! Lift and carry!'

Davey and Lisa skirted round the pairs of children tottering in from the dining room.

'Hold it.' Mr Craddock said as they walked past. 'Let's have a look.' Davey held up the lantern for his inspection. 'Hmm. It'll do, I suppose.' Lisa grinned and winked. 'Put it over there with the others,' Craddock added.

A big table by the window held a long row of orange globes of all sizes, from small to huge. They looked good all together. Davey put his with the medium ones and stood back to admire the overall effect.

'Much more to do, Sir?' Lisa asked Mr Craddock.

'Nearly there, Lisa. Nearly there,' the teacher replied, running his hand through his hair.

He did look considerably harassed. His normally neat dark hair was standing on end from where he had been raking his fingers through it, and his shirt was hanging out at the back, but the room was looking impressive. Another class was doing the catering, but decorating it had been 7JC's responsibility. The colour scheme was orange and black. Bats clung to windows and walls, witches rode from ceiling to floor. Football nets hung down like spiders' webs, some containing nests of black and orange balloon eggs. Cut-out letters strung across the room proclaimed WEL-COME TO THE HALLOWE'N DISCO.

Mr Craddock let out a howl when Lisa pointed out the spelling mistake and raced off to find the missing E. Once that was in place, everything would be perfect.

Davey was glad the room looked good. Tom and Elinor were coming tonight, and Kate would also be putting in an appearance, perhaps with some of her friends from the first year of the Senior part of the school. He didn't want them sneering, saying the disco was sad and pathetic just because they were older than him.

'Can we light the candles, Sir?' someone asked when everything was finished.

'Please, Sir.'

'Go on, Sir.'

'Go on.'

Pleading came from all sides, but Craddock looked uncertain. He did not reply at first and faces fell, anticipating refusal.

'We-ell . . . All right, then,' he suddenly smiled, 'I don't see why not.'

Several boys leaped forward, one with a Zippo lighter, others with matches.

'I don't know where you got those from.' Mr Craddock frowned his disapproval. 'You shouldn't be bringing them into school. *I'll* do it.'

The teacher stepped up to the table and, one by one, ignited the little night-lights inside the pumpkins. Some didn't take straight away, but soon they were all glowing well.

'Lights, someone!' the teacher ordered, and one of the pupils obliged by flicking off the hall's overhead lights.

The class crowded round to admire their handiwork. No one had really noticed until now, but outside the dark was coming on. It had been a gloomy day and the last of the light was beginning to fade, the dark, grey clouds deepening to indigo. The class chatter died down and one or two pupils shivered as the wind whined in the telegraph wires, swirling the last of the leaves down from the trees, setting branches tap-tapping against the window. All eyes were focused on the warm glow spilling from lanterns as individual as the people who had made them. Orange light poured from triangular eyes and snouts, radiating out of menacing grins and crooked, jagged, snarling mouths.

The purpose of the lanterns, as the class had learnt earlier in the day, was to protect the bearer from evil spirits. Would these be enough to protect them all from whatever walked abroad, whatever stalked the living world, on this night of all nights?

Outside the wind seemed to intensify. Several more children shivered and drew closer together as a little gust sneaked right into the room beside them. A couple of the lanterns guttered, Davey's among them. The others flared back up, resuming their brightness; but Davey's stayed dark, the only gap in the cheery glowing line.

At that moment, the bell went. Mr Craddock began directing work afresh and those who were not involved collected their lanterns and went off to the cloakrooms.

'See you tonight, then?' Lisa said when they got outside. 'At the disco?'

'Yeah,' Davey replied. 'We're going trick-or-treating first. Kate and me and my cousins. Want to come?' he added as an afterthought.

'Yeah, sure. What time?'

'Our house. About seven?'

'Right,' she smiled, 'I'll be there. Thanks, Davey.'

'No problem. Bring your lantern. Mine's not much use. It keeps fizzling out.'

He held his darkened lantern up against hers. Lisa's was still going strong, orange light spilling out into the darkening night.

'Never mind,' she shrugged. 'Yours probably hasn't got enough air inside.'

'Maybe.' Davey lifted the lid and peered in.

'Have you tried lighting it again?'

'Yeah. Billy Hawking lent me his matches. Still nothing.' Davey frowned and bit his lip. He was beginning to look worried.

'Hey, don't get upset. Craddock didn't say they *had* to light, did he?'

'No, it's not that. It's . . .'

'It's what?'

'Nothing.' Davey shook his head, unable to explain.

'Never mind.' Lisa gave him a puzzled smile. 'It doesn't matter.' Sometimes Davey could be strange, but that was one of the things she liked about him. 'I'll see you later. 'Bye, Davey.'

'Yeah, 'bye Lise. See you.'

Lisa hitched up her rucksack and went off, lantern swinging, into the gathering night. Davey knew it was silly to be concerned just because his stupid pumpkin refused to light. Lisa was probably right. It was all to do

139

with oxygen and scientific stuff like that. But in class earlier they had been talking about omens, Hallowe'en was a time for them. For seeing what was good – or bad.

Davey had been looking forward to Hallowe'en for weeks: trick-or-treat, the disco, the twins coming. There were other aspects to the festival, though. Some of these gave him the shivers and made the small hairs creep up the back of his neck.

Tonight was a special time, Craddock had said so in that morning's lesson. For thousands of years, this period had been associated with ghosts and spirits and with death. A time when the barriers between this world and the next went down and the dead could return from the grave. Beings from other worlds were free to walk among the living. At this, some of the class had made 'woo, wooing' noises and snorted with laughter; for them Hallowe'en meant playing tricks and eating sweets. Davey stayed quiet, because he knew that such things *could* occur.

The Haunts Ghost Tour he had taken at midsummer, with Kate, Tom and Elinor, was still fresh in his mind. Strange things had happened. Somehow they had slipped into another, parallel, world, and met with a cast of characters, ghosts and creatures so bizarre that Davey sometimes thought he must have dreamt them: Jack Cade, the highwayman, and his ghost crew: Polly, the inn keeper's daughter; the girl, Elizabeth; the mute boy, Govan; the Blind Fiddler – they had proved good and kind. But the ghost city was home to other crews:

terrifying creatures steeped in ancient malice, with no love for the living. Good or bad, these beings had one thing in common: they were all dead. Davey had told no one else about this experience. Tom, Elinor and Kate had not discussed it afterwards. But Davey knew it had happened. He knew that it was no dream, and he no longer scoffed when people spoke of ghosts.

Davey looked down at his darkened lantern and shivered, crossing his fingers and sending up a quick wish. No matter what he *wanted* to think, he had a feeling that his light going out *was* an omen, and a bad one. It did not bode well for the night ahead. What had happened once, could happen again.

2

'*She's* not coming with us, is she?' Davey asked when he got home.

His younger sister, Emma, was standing in the hall in her ghost outfit, white sheet over her head.

'Mum said I could.' Blue eyes gleamed with resentment through ragged black-rimmed holes.

Davey went into the kitchen.

'Is that right, Mum? You said Emma could come?'

'I can, can't I?' The ghost had followed him through. She was flapping her arms now, billowing the sheeting. 'I'm old enough this year to go trickle treating . . .'

Davey rolled his eyes to the ceiling. 'It's trick *or* treating. How often do you have to be told?'

'It won't do any harm, Davey.' His mother turned from the sink, drying her hands on a cloth. 'There's three of you to take care of her. As long as you stick to the local streets. She's been so looking forward to it . . .'

'What does Kate think?'

'Katie's not bothered,' Emma answered for her sister. 'She's not mean like you and she's the eldest.'

She swerved away, flapping and screeching, as Davey took a half-playful swipe at her.

'Now, now,' his mother frowned at him. 'You can stop that.'

'She started it,' Davey said, arms folded. 'What about the disco after?'

'I'm coming to that, too.'

Davey groaned. 'You can't. You're too small.'

'Not any more,' his mother pointed out. 'Not since she moved up to the Juniors. The ticket says all ages invited and she paid for it herself out of her own pocket money. Don't be rotten, Davey. What's the matter with you, anyway? Bad day at school?'

'Not particularly,' Davey muttered. He couldn't explain what was really on his mind and he could hardly say he was in a bad mood because his Hallowe'en lantern wouldn't light properly. Neither could he admit to one of Gran's 'funny feelings' again; her 'premonitions' were a joke throughout the family.

'Good. Because your cousins will be arriving shortly and I don't want you all moody and sulky. Why don't you go and get your room ready? Clear a little corner of the pigsty for Tom.'

'It's not that bad!'

'Oh?' His mother looked down at him. 'Did an army of cleaners go in as soon as I went off to work?'

'Oh, OK,' Davey turned to go. 'You can take that stupid thing off for now,' he said to his sister as he left the kitchen. 'We're not going yet.'

★   ★   ★

'I'll get it!'

Davey ran down the stairs to answer the door, his face brown and green, his rubber Terror of the Crypt mask in his hand. He was wearing mud-covered trousers and one of his dad's old shirts daubed with ketchup blood stains, and grey paint graveyard slime.

Tom and Elinor had arrived. They had not seen Davey or Kate since midsummer and Davey was determined to ask them about what had happened on the Haunts Ghost Tour. But it didn't look as if there would be time this evening. First Mum was fussing all over them, stuffing tea down them and demanding to know how things were at home; then Kate wanted both of them to join her upstairs to get ready for trick-or-treating. Any discussion would have to wait until later.

The house was in chaos. Kate and Ellie were giggling away in Kate's bedroom trying on costumes and experimenting with make-up. Tom was trying to repair his Frankenstein's Monster mask with a stapler. Mum and Dad were rushing around getting ready to go out to their own fancy dress party and Emma was haunting the landing, practising 'Oohing' noises.

The bell rang again.

'I'm coming. I'm coming.'

Davey opened the door and the words of greeting died in his mouth.

First he saw a pumpkin lantern, its malevolent grin lit by a flickering light from within. Above that a black cloak shrouded a skeletal figure, the face beneath the hood showed wide, grinning teeth, an eroded nose and empty eye sockets. Skeleton hands shot out. Davey jumped back as the wide sleeves fell back to show bones, white to the elbow. He could feel himself sweating. This creature, this *thing* reminded him of something . . .

'Trick or treat, Davey Williams?' a voice intoned, rasping, harsh, gravelly with menace. 'Choose well. Choose swiftly. For I am come.'

'It's only me.' Lisa pulled her skull mask off. 'What's up?' She grinned. 'You look like you've seen a ghost.'

'Nothing.' Davey looked away feeling himself redden. 'I just got a bit hot in my costume, that's all.' He turned to the stairs. 'I'll tell the others that you're here.'

Cruella DeVille and Count Dracula stood in the hall dishing out orders to a small ghost, two witches, Frankenstein's Monster, a black robed skeleton and the Terror from the Crypt.

'You look nice, Mum,' the Terror said. The long gown and glittery jewellery made her look very glamorous.

'Thank you, Davey.' His mother arched her thin black brows and gave him a red-lipsticked smile. 'Now, make sure you bring Emma back at a reasonable time.' She smoothed back the silver streak in the front of her long dark hair. 'Zoe should be along to babysit around nine. If there are any problems, you can contact us on this number.'

145

'We don't need a babysitter,' Kate objected as her mother wrote a number on the pad next to the phone. 'We're old enough to look after ourselves.'

Kate was thirteen and thought of herself as all but grown up.

'That's a matter of opinion,' her mother replied. 'Legally, and in my opinion, you're not – but it's my opinion that counts.'

'Are witches supposed to wear that much make-up to go out?' Her father asked.

'You're a fine one to talk.' Kate grinned up at his chalk-white face and red lips. 'The answer is: they are if they're going straight to a disco afterwards.'

She glanced at her reflection in the hall mirror. She and Elinor had worked from a Scary Glamour feature in a magazine. The results were pretty good. Neither of them wanted to go looking exactly like a genuine fright. Unlike Lisa. Kate surveyed Davey's friend's rubber features – Lisa had obviously just gone for 'scary'.

'And no nicking those,' Mr Williams nodded towards the dish of sweets on the table under the mirror. 'Those are for the kids coming here. Go and get some of your own. I thought that was the whole idea?'

'Everyone got their bags to put the stuff in?' Kate said as they got outside.

They all nodded, fidgeting from foot to foot, more from nerves and excitement than the need to keep warm.

The night was windy, but not cold. It held no threat of rain. Above the orange glow of the street lights, the silver sliver of the new moon was flitting in and out of dark clouds, scudding across the sky.

'We keep to the local streets. We're just going to do the estate.' Kate went through the rules. 'And no scoffing everything we get. The idea is that it is supposed to be kept and shared out after. And Emma?' She turned from the rest of them to specifically address her little sister. 'You are not to eat anything, *anything at all*, unless I've checked it out. Is that clear?'

'Yes,' Emma said in a quiet little voice. Sometimes Kate sounded a lot like Mrs Bevan, her teacher.

'OK. Let's go.'

The Williams family lived on the Puckeridge Estate. One of a series of new developments which had grown up round the ancient settlement of Wesson Heath. The centre of the village was still quaint, with an old church and a village green ringed by thatched cottages and half-timbered pubs; but the outskirts had been transformed.

Wesson Heath was a bustling place. Apart from the new housing estates, there was the Norwood retail and business park. The city grew bigger each year, eating up more and more of the green open space, the old heath, which gave the village its name, the common land and fields, changing the nature of the place, destroying a history which stretched back to Saxon times and before.

It was Kate's idea to start at the top of their estate and

work down the winding curve of drives and closes. The estate was divided by two long, gently sloping avenues leading in from right and left: Puckridge Rise, named after the estate, led into Derry Way which ended in a cul-de-sac next to the big old house at the bottom. In between these two main roads, others curled in and round each other. The builders had been keen to cram in as many houses as possible, emphasising the rural setting by giving the streets names such as Garden Court, Orchard Close, Meadow Drive, Springfield Avenue. Each name recalled the function of the land that the new houses were built upon. Derry House stood on its own in an area still referred to as the Hollow, even though this name appeared on no street sign. From there it was a quick walk across the fields to the school. Once there, they would stow their swag in Kate's locker to divvy out later and head for the disco.

Kate was just explaining this when Davey noticed another gang of trick or treaters heading towards them. The leader was small, dressed like a Ku Klux Klansman in a dirty white robe painted with a red cross. He had his hood thrown back and as they went past, his eyes gleamed out of a hideous pale rubber mask, at least Davey assumed it was a mask, and the mouth creased in a grin of recognition. Davey could not place him, but it could be anybody inside that outfit, maybe it was a kid from school. He was followed by a monk dressed in a hooded black habit and a lookalike for Pennywise, the clown in

Stephen King's *IT*, who was carrying a shiny red balloon on a stick.

'They're doing our street. What a cheek!'

'Never mind. Plenty for everyone.' Kate turned left into Tinker's Drive. 'Let's get started.'

Davey followed her up the first path and stood back as she knocked on the door ready to chant:

> *Hey-ho for Hallowe'en,*
> *All the witches to be seen.*
> *Some in black and some in green,*
> *Hey-ho for Hallowe'en!*
> *Trick or Treat!*

The rhyme was pretty cheesy, but it was all part of Kate's strategy. She reckoned that it was like carol singing: you got more if you gave them a bit of a verse first.

Davey was round the corner accepting the first treats of the evening, so he didn't see the other crew walk past all the other houses until they got to his pathway. He didn't know that they knocked on his door only. Neither did he see them disappear inside, to make their own selection from the plate left out for visiting ghosts and ghouls.

3

'Hang on a sec.'

Davey sat on a wall to empty his trainer. The last house had a drive thick with newly-laid gravel and Davey seemed to have got most of it in his shoes. They were on Derry Way nearing the bottom of the Hollow. To the left stood the gates to Derry House, to the right lay the path to the school. While he was at it, he had a quick look in his bag. Not a bad haul. Mini Mars Bars and Bounties, a box of Poppets, a bag of nuts, a couple of Tazs and some chews. He dug out a chew, strawberry, his favourite. Kate and the others had gone round the corner, so Davey reckoned it was safe to unwrap it and pop it in his mouth. He screwed up the wrapper and put it in his pocket. One wouldn't hurt after all.

He was just about to follow them, when he noticed a movement near Derry House. Two figures were going up the wide stone steps to the big front door. They looked like Emma and Lisa, one in white, the other in black. Derry House was big – a rambling mansion that lay at the centre of the estate. All the drives and closes had been built on its grounds and gardens. The house had originally been called The Dwerry House after the place where it had been built, Dwerry Holes. The 'w' had been dropped, lost along the way. The 'holes', a system of underground chambers and tunnels, left over from old flint works and quarrying, had long ago been filled in and the place had become known as the Hollow. Few remembered the change of name, or knew that it came from *dwerg*, an old English word meaning *Dwarf* or *Changeling*. The original name had been given out of fear and superstition, but few people believe in such things now.

The house itself was very large. The front was Victorian, but other parts were far older and made of light grey stone. Different wings and bits had been added in different periods, giving the house a rambling, higgledy-piggledy appearance.

After the new estate had been built, Derry House itself had stood empty for a long time before being converted into an old people's home. The owners had failed to make a go of it. Davey was not surprised. It was surrounded by high evergreen trees and bushes and even on the brightest of days it had a dark gloomy feel. Estate agents' boards proclaimed it 'ripe for new development'. Right now, no one lived in it, Davey was sure of that.

It might as well have had a banner reading 'Haunted House' slung across the front of it. The red brick facade, with its tall windows, round turrets and steeply-pitched gables, made the place look like every creepy house in every spooky film you had ever seen. It was not the kind of place to visit in broad daylight, let alone at night. And tonight of all nights: '*when the veil separating the dead from the living is at its thinnest . . .*' A quote came back from Craddock's lesson. It had sounded scary even in the brightly-lit classroom.

Davey stood at the top of the long, sloping drive, unable to believe his eyes. What were they doing? And if that was Emma and Lisa he could see, where were the others? He was just about to shout out a warning when the door opened and the two figures went in.

He stood for a moment, undecided, then he steeled himself to venture down the drive. Big wooden gates drooping on rusting hinges were permanently secured back above an empty expanse of tarmac which was cracked and buckled by tree roots and the blind white heads of fungi.

Thick pads of moss cushioned his feet as he entered the shadow of the tall gaunt house. Big windows bulged out, looking down at him with blank eyes. Davey could feel his courage failing. He did not know where the others were, and had no idea what could make Lisa and Emma go into such a scary place. He swallowed his own fear down. They were his little sister and his best friend. He could not allow them to go alone.

He stepped into the porch. Black paint was peeling and bare wood showed on the barley twist pillars which held up the roof. Davey went up the cracked stone steps and rang the small modern buzzer set into the door frame. No sound came from inside so he tried the tarnished brass knocker. He banged, once, twice. The sound went out, booming and hollow, but there was no need to wait for an answer, the door was open . . .

The door creaked as it swung away from him. He stood, hesitating on the threshold, reluctant to enter. It was very dark inside. Bare boards stretched away for a few metres before being swallowed in the blackness of the wide hall and staircase. Davey shouted out for Lisa and Emma, but there was no reply, only his own voice calling back to him, frightened and small. Davey nearly turned on his heels, but he was kept by the idea of them being here, he'd seen them go in, after all.

He entered the hall. At first, he wished he had a torch with him, but the first room brought second thoughts. It was OK in TV series, to have long shafts of light poking into corners, but right now Davey didn't want to know what might be hiding there.

Street lighting, filtering through the curtainless dusty windows, showed the first room to be empty. This must have been the dining room. It still smelt faintly of stale cabbage and shepherd's pie. Davey tried not to think of all the creepy stories he knew about this house, why it had stayed so long deserted, all the things that were supposed to have happened here. Instead he thought about all the old dears sitting here eating, but then another thought struck him. Never mind what had happened in the house before, loads of *them* must have died here since then. The whole place could be bristling . . .

As if on cue, a sound came from the next room. Davey felt the hairs rising along his skin and up the back of his neck. Very carefully, very quietly, but with his own heart drumming, and the breath whistling in and out of him, he retraced his footsteps, leaving the door open to give as much light as possible.

He trod down the corridor and with shaking hand pushed open the door. He fully expected to see Lisa and Emma. He was even bracing himself for them to jump out at him, but there was nobody.

A muffled scuffling came from somewhere behind him. First on the stair and then on the landing, like someone light footed running upstairs. It was followed by stifled laughter, high-pitched giggling . . .

'Emma! Lisa!'

Davey's fear was turning to anger and he leapt up the stairs two at a time, his terror forgotten. They were playing tricks. His friend and his little sister. How could they do that to him?

As he reached the first turn of the stairs, the laughter redoubled and seemed to be joined by other voices. High pitched but stronger, probably Kate or Elinor and a male voice, deeper, gruffer. That must be Tom. They were all in it together. They had lured him in here, frightened him half to death, and now they were taking the . . .

Davey was beside himself with fury. He roared out their names and a string of curses as he leapt across the second landing and up the next flight of stairs. The mocking laughter was tinged with more than a hint of cruelty, and was getting louder, building as if in anticipation . . .

Davey followed the sounds, his anger blanketing everything, blotting out other senses that might have warned him of what might be waiting. The stairs became steeper, narrower, leading up to the attic. Davey stood on the final landing, panting. This area had none of the grandeur of the rest of the house. It was small and poky and smelt musty with damp and decay. A dusty skylight let in a small amount of dingy light from the low sloping roof. The plaster was cracked and falling. Davey stepped across the landing. The floor was gritty with crumbled rubble and dried mouse droppings. Three doors faced him. One straight ahead, a few steps in front of him, two off to the side, one left, one right.

He stopped and listened before taking another step forward. There was nothing to indicate which door to open. The laughing and giggling had ceased. There was no sound at all, only his own footsteps crunching over the bare boards. Davey stopped again to listen. The silence was absolute, but filled with suffocating tension, a terrible, trembling anticipation, as if the house itself was holding its breath.

Davey risked another step forward, until he was right

up to the door facing him. He put his ear to it, and then he did hear something. Very faint, very quiet. Someone crying to themselves. It sounded like a young child. It could be Emma. Maybe the others had brought her up here and left her, or maybe she had got separated somehow and the house, the game, the tension had all got too much for her.

Davey put his hand on the door and pushed. It swung inwards on to a narrow room with a steeply-pitched roof. Huddled in the corner was a small figure dressed in white.

'It's OK, Emma,' Davey said, going forward, arms outstretched to comfort her. 'I'm here now. It's all right . . .'

He was nearly there when the figure whirled round. Davey's heart lurched. The face was hideously ugly, greyish-green in the weak light, gnarled and wrinkled. The rubbery features creased and twisted in a leering grin as the figure leapt towards him. The creature was short, not much taller than Emma, but the arms reaching for Davey were thick and powerful, the hands about to grab him were hairy like a man's.

'Trick or treat, Davey Williams?' The words came slurring and gutteral through liver-coloured lips. 'Trick or treat?'

Davey had seen him before, he'd been one of the group out on their street. Repulsed, Davey jumped backwards, reaching behind him for the open door, stumbling out on to the landing. Either side a door

156

was opening. The clown stepped out, his red suit billowing dark, his dead white face, shining leprous in the faint light, grinning triumph. A black-robed figure came from the other side, gliding and silent. Davey felt the breath of the graveyard on his face. This was no rubber mask above a painted suit, the grinning skull and skeletal hands were real.

Davey let out a cry, somewhere between a shriek and a squeak. He felt the blood thud and sing in his head. These were no ordinary trick-or-treaters, they must be some kind of ghost crew.

It was now or never. If he did not move he would be lost forever. Davey lunged forward, somehow managing to slip between them. He hurled himself down the stairs, skidding round the landings, tumbling and slipping down the worn treadless steps. He could hear them shuffling and scuffling behind him as he fled helter-skelter on legs turned to rubber with terror. At the bottom of the third flight, he lost his footing and hurtled forward, propelled by his own momentum. Only purest instinct saved him. At the last minute, he put out a hand, sensing the emptiness in front of his face.

At some time in the past a lift had been installed to take residents up and down stairs. Since then the mechanism had been removed. On other floors sliding doors scissored across, guarding the unwary from the empty shaft, but this one had been concertinaed back. Davey gripped on to the metal frame, sweaty hands slipping, and swung out into nothing. He hung for a second above the black void. A cold draft of air came straight up from the basement, with it came a woman's laughter. He risked a glance down as the eerie sound intensified and saw eyes looking up at him, silver in the darkness. There was something in the house besides the ghost crew. Something, or someone, was down there waiting for him.

He let out a high whistling shriek of terror and just about managed to swing himself back again. He flattened himself against the wall, his whole body shaking, sweat pouring down his sides, his heart hammering in his chest.

The three figures were ranged across the stairs, coming down towards him. They stepped on to the landing, one at a time, in no hurry now, thinking that they had him trapped. The clown came forward, arms folded, fat white gloves lost in the dark red folds of his baggy suit.

'There's someone wanting to see you.' Dark little teeth showed in his grinning mouth. 'A lady of some importance. It wouldn't do to keep a lady waiting, now would it? No more running, no more chasing.' He was very close now, speaking in a whisper, the words hissing out of him. 'You'd better—'

A sound from downstairs stopped him in mid-sentence. The big front door creaked open and banged back against the wall.

'Davey?' Tom's voice came up the stairs, echoing loud through the silence of the house. 'Are you in here?'

'. . . couldn't be.' Kate's voice sounded fainter, as if from outside. 'Even Davey wouldn't be that stupid.'

'I am.' Davey managed to squeak. 'I'm up here, Tom. Up here!'

He never knew if Tom heard him, but the interruption was enough to keep the ghost crew at bay and allow Davey to get away. He lurched forwards, leaping down the rest of the stairs, surfing the last remaining treads until he was in the hall. He hurled himself on from there, grabbing his cousin by the arm and pulling both of them out through the front door. Their exit was followed by a deep hissing down draft of icy air, like someone opening a vacuum pack. Davey dragged Tom down the steps. Behind them the front door slammed shut.

Kate stood with Elinor looking up at the house; behind them stood two smaller figures, one in white and one in black.

'What on earth were you doing in there?' Kate shouted, her relief at finding him again rapidly turning to anger.

'Nothing. Come on.' Davey began to run up the drive. He didn't want to stand there arguing. They needed to get away from there. They had to get clear.

'What made you go in, Davey?' Kate asked when she caught up with him.

'I don't know. I thought I saw . . .'

'Saw who?'

'Emma and Lisa, by the door. Then I thought maybe you'd all—'

'Gone into the house?' Kate finished for him. 'But we wouldn't do that, Davey. Because we're not crazy!' She screwed a finger into the side of her head to emphasise the point. 'For goodness' sake, you're worse than Emma sometimes. Now don't go wandering off again. Follow me!'

'Kate. Wait up. There's something else . . .' Davey shouted, but she marched off with Elinor before he could say anything else to her, leading them all on towards the school.

Davey followed, falling in beside Tom.

'Did you do it for a dare?' Tom grinned, his Frankenstein face creased in admiration.

'Not exactly . . . Tom, there's something—'

'Takes some guts to go in there . . .' Tom interrupted, shaking his head in wonder. 'Well done, mate!'

'But I didn't do it for that reason! Tom, stop a minute.' Davey caught hold of his arm. 'You've got to listen! Do you remember this summer? When you came down for your birthdays?'

'Yeah. We went for a pizza. What about it?'

'No! We went on the Haunts Ghost Tour, don't you remember?'

Tom frowned at Davey. Perhaps Kate was right. Perhaps he *had* gone crazy. Something must have happened in that house to fry his cousin's brains. Tom had no idea what he was babbling on about.

'Yes, you do! You must!' Davey went on, desperate now. 'We met these people, except they weren't real people.'

'What were they then?'

'They were—'

'What are you two whispering about?'

Lisa had dropped back and she was looking at them sharply, head on one side, eyes bright with curiosity. He could never explain with her there. She would not believe a word of it. She was the most sceptical person he had ever met, she had laughed louder than the boys at Craddock's Hallowe'en scare stories. To make matters worse she had Emma with her. Davey closed his eyes. There was no way he could talk to Tom now.

'Nothing,' he muttered.

'Good,' Emma chimed in, 'because Kate says to stop dawdling about. Come on, Davey.' She slipped her arm through his. 'We've got to hurry up. The disco will be over before we even get there and I've never been to one before.'

Davey allowed himself to be pulled down the path towards the school. Music came thumping across the playground and fields and through the picket fence he could see that the place was all lit up. Davey quickened his step. The disco had already started and he wanted to get in among the lights, music, people. Judging from Tom's reaction, he would have a tough time explaining what had happened in Derry House. But nothing could happen here, surely?

4

Wesson Heath School Hall was filling up nicely, but there were more kids running about than dancing. Emma went off to join a posse of miniature Draculas, devils and ghouls and was soon racing round happily, screaming her head off. Kate took Tom and Elinor over to meet her friends who were all in one corner trying to look cool. Which left Davey and Lisa on their own.

'Why did you go in there, Davey?' Lisa asked as they leaned against the wall. 'Into Derry House, I mean.'

'I don't know . . .'

'Yes, you do,' Lisa said, she knew when he was hiding something. 'I want to know.'

'Well,' Davey replied, trying to think what to say. Lisa was a good friend. He didn't want to lie to her, so he decided to tell as much of the truth as he could. 'If you must know,' he said after a while, 'I thought I saw you and Em go in, and, and I couldn't let you be there on your own, could I?'

'I suppose not. Why did you think it was us?'

'I saw two figures. From a distance they looked like they were wearing the same kind of costumes.'

'Must have been some other kids out trick-or-treating.'

'Yeah.' Davey nodded a little too quickly. 'I guess.'

'Was it scary? In the house, I mean.'

Davey was just about to say, 'Of course not', but even remembering made him shiver. Who were those freaks inside Derry House? He could not have imagined anything that horrible . . .

'Yes,' he said quietly. 'Yes, it really was.'

Lisa looked at him closely. There were things he still wasn't telling her but, if that's what he wanted, fair enough. He could get very stubborn, and she knew not to push him. It was, after all, his own business.

'Well, I think it was very brave of you to go in there,' she said finally. 'Whatever the reason, it was a brave thing to do.'

'Thanks, Lise.' Davey was surprised. Lisa didn't usually hand out compliments.

'Yeah, well. Just thought I'd say . . . Hey, have you seen Craddock?' she added, her eyes suddenly bright with mischief.

Davey glanced around, grateful for the change of subject. The tall, dark-haired teacher was stalking the room, ticking off the more boisterous disco goers, and picking up fallen balloons.

'What is he dressed as?'

Craddock was carrying a crumpled top hat and wearing a short cloak over a frock coat.

'Jekyll and Hyde, I think,' Lisa replied. 'The scowl's his own, but he's dressed like a Victorian and he's got a stethoscope.'

'Pretty good outfit.' Davey nodded. 'Really suits him.'

'Not as good as Parsons, look at her!'

Lisa pointed out the Deputy Head. She was a large fearsome looking woman at the best of times, with strong hawk-like features and black hair streaked with grey. She usually wore her hair up in a bun, but now it streamed down her back from under a tall black conical hat. Her black cloak and skirts swirled and her face glowed green and purple in the flashing disco lighting as she strode round the room, quelling the over-excited at a glance and discouraging unruly behaviour with the business end of her broomstick.

'Now that is typecasting!'

Lisa laughed, 'I dare you to go and tell her, "*It's fancy dress. You aren't supposed to come as yourself!*" '

Davey laughed too, grateful to Lisa for lightening his mood.

'Come on,' he said. 'Let's find the others. See what's happening.'

He took Lisa to join the others in their class. Some of the girls were out on the dancefloor, going through their routines. Lisa persuaded Davey and some of the boys to join in and soon they were all messing around, calling out requests to the DJ, having a laugh.

The music was loud, more and more people were dancing. Mrs Parsons had long ago given up trying to stop the little ones charging round, confining herself to preventing them escaping from the hall to rampage round the school. The atmosphere was steamy, mist forming over the dancers, condensation pouring down the walls. Davey was beginning to feel very hot inside his Terror of the Crypt suit.

'Fancy a drink?' he said to Lisa when he could catch her. 'I'm gasping.'

'Sure.' She separated herself from a long unruly line of dancing girls. 'Let's grab a Coke.'

The refreshment tables were up one end. They were manned by other members of staff and pupils from the upper school. One table held snacks and cans for sale. The food and drink on the other one was free, courtesy of the school and 7HD. The sign above read: *Gruesome Grub*.

5

Bowls of Monster Munch flanked plates of stuff made and labelled by 7HD: *Frankenstein's Spares, Snot Clots, Deadmen's Eyeballs, Mummy's Fingers, Dracula Jelly* and *Vampire Blood*. Davey swallowed hard. It all looked pretty unappetising but, because it was free, plenty were tucking in. Lisa took a plate and helped herself.

'Umm,' she bit into an Eyeball. 'These are pretty good. Do you want to try one?'

Davey shook his head.

'They're only dyed potato balls. I was in there when they were making them. Here, have one. Try a Mummy's Finger. It's sausage, really.'

Davey did not want people to think he had been put off by 7HD's disgusting labels. He picked up the food Lisa offered and bit into it saying to himself, 'green dyed potato, skinless sausage'.

He immediately regretted what he had done. Salt slime seemed to coat his tongue. As he chewed the grey–pink flesh, his teeth grated on bits of bone and gristle. Saliva flooded his mouth and his tea backed up in his throat. He thought he was going to be sick. He looked round desperately and then spat the whole mess out in a bin full of crisp bags.

'I didn't think they were that bad,' Lisa said, considering. 'Here. You'd better have a drink.'

Lisa handed him a plastic cup. Davey took a big gulp. The thick salty liquid was warm and tasted faintly metallic. It clung to the side of the cup, staining the polystyrene . . .

Davey made a bolt for the boys' toilets. This time he really was going to throw up.

He came back, pale beneath his brown and green make-up.

'It's only blackcurrant!' Lisa picked up another cup of Dracula's blood and swilled it round. 'Smell it!'

She took a sniff and held it up to him.

Davey wiped his mouth and turned away. 'I'd rather not. Thanks very much.'

He wanted to get away from the food-laden table. Even the smell was enough to turn his stomach. He had not imagined it. The food and drink had transformed in his mouth into something utterly disgusting, but no one else seemed affected. He looked around at his classmates happily scoffing and began to feel sick again. Why had it only happened to him?

Davey would not have admitted it, but he was glad when it was time to go. The lights and noise were giving him a headache and he still felt kind of queasy. It came as a relief when Kate announced that it was 'boring' and they had to get Emma home.

They walked back a different way so they could drop

Lisa off at her house. She invited them in, but Emma had to be back by eight-thirty at the latest.

'See you, then,' Lisa waved and began to walk down her drive.

'Yeah. Monday,' Davey replied.

'It's half-term,' Tom reminded him.

'Oh, yeah. Maybe we could do something?'

Lisa smiled. 'Great. Give me a call.'

'OK.' Davey waved and walked away.

'You're doing all right there, mate,' Tom commented as they went down the street. 'She's not bad looking. Not bad at all!'

'She's just a friend.' Davey turned on him. 'Don't be stupid!'

Tom carried on grinning as Davey looked round defiantly at the others. Kate raised an eyebrow at Elinor but didn't say anything.

'What's the matter, Davey?' Emma fell back to keep him company as the others moved on.

'Nothing.' He looked down at her and took her hand.

'When can we eat the trickle treat sweets?'

'When we get home.'

'Come on, then.' She pulled him forward. 'Let's go.'

They walked along, hand in hand. Emma chattered all the way to the end of their drive, and then she stopped.

'Look, Davey,' she said. 'Look at that.'

'What?' He glanced around, trying to see what had caught her attention.

'This balloon.' She picked a red balloon on a stick out of the hedge at the top of their path. 'Isn't it pretty? Maybe it's come from school.'

'Maybe, but those were all black or orange, I'm pretty sure, and they were rubber. This is metallic . . .'

'Can I keep it?'

'I don't see why not . . .' Davey said, and immediately regretted his words. Emma had a firm grasp on it, there would be no getting it off her now but, as she turned it round, Davey saw that it was painted with a crude clown face. The balloon bobbled about of its own accord, weighted inside with something heavy. Davey put out a finger to touch it. One of the black cross-eyes seemed to wink and the fat mouth widened into a grin as it nodded back and forth . . .

'Hey, look.'

'Where?' Davey searched around wondering what else she might have found.

'Down there,' Emma pointed. 'Someone's taken sweets from our house and stomped them into the ground.'

Davey looked down at the flattened wrappers and oozing contents.

'How do you know they're from our house?'

'Pick 'n' Mix from Woolworth's. I was with Mum when she bought them. I helped her put them out. Now here they are squashed and broken.' Emma stared down at the ground frowning, and then looked up at her brother. 'Who would do a thing like that?'

6

Mum and Dad had already gone out and there was no sign of Zoe who was supposed to be babysitting. She was not expected until nine, and it was still only eight forty-five. No need to worry. Yet.

'She'll be along later, I expect,' Kate said, taking charge. 'Emma, you get ready for bed.'

'I haven't had my sweets yet.'

'OK. But don't eat them all now. You'll be sick. Save some for the morning.'

They divided them up on the kitchen table.

'Can I stay down here with you?' Emma mumbled through a mouthful of chocolate.

'I don't think that would be a good idea,' Kate replied. 'Mum said you weren't to be too late and it's way past your bedtime as it is. Finish what you've got in your mouth and then go and wash your face and clean your teeth.'

'What do you fancy doing?' Kate asked when Emma went upstairs.

'How about watching a video?'

'Great idea. Except we haven't got one out. And the shop will be shut by now.'

'Just so happens I've got the very thing.' Tom reached in his backpack.

'What?'

'Guess.'

'Can't.' Kate shook her head.

'*Halloween*, what do you think? And *Halloween 2*. They come on the same video.'

'Let's have a look.' Kate held her hand out for the film. 'Hey, cool! Where did you get them?'

'A mate. His brother's a real horror-film freak. He let me take my pick.'

'It's an 18.' Davey said, looking at the cover. He did not like the way this was going. 'Mum and Dad wouldn't be happy.'

'How are they going to know? They aren't here, are they?'

'What about Zoe?'

'She's not here, either. Anyway, she won't care. She'll watch it with us, I should think.' Kate frowned at her brother. 'What's your problem, Davey?'

'I don't know.' Davey shook his head. 'I just don't want to watch it.'

'What's the matter? Scared?'

'No. Who went in Derry House?'

'That wasn't brave,' Kate commented. 'That was just stupid. What about you two? Do you want to see it?'

Tom and Elinor shrugged, 'Of course. We brought it.'

'That settles it. You don't have to watch it, if you don't want to, Davey.'

★　　★　　★

172

Emma came back downstairs then, making it difficult for Davey to explain why he did not want to watch the video. He was not nervous about the content, he'd watched worse than that. Mum would go ape if she found out, especially with no babysitter and Emma still about, but Davey wasn't concerned about parental consent. There was just this feeling inside of him, and it was growing stronger by the minute: watching a film like that tonight would not be a wise thing to do.

Tom was setting up the video. I'll have to say something soon, Davey thought, as he went into the kitchen to help get snacks and drinks organised. There were things they needed to talk about, like what had happened on the Haunts Ghost Tour; what was happening now in Derry House. Forces were gathering out there, Davey shivered, which would make the psycho in *Halloween* look like nothing.

'Can I stay and have some?' Emma asked as Ellie put pizza in to warm and Davey kept an eye on batches of popcorn pop popping away in the microwave.

'No,' Kate replied. 'You've cleaned your teeth and, besides, you've eaten enough junk for one night, any more and your tummy will be poorly. It's really time for bed.'

'I was waiting for someone to come and tuck me in.' Emma took a handful of popcorn. 'Where's Zoe?'

'Not here yet.'

'She's awfully late.'

Kate frowned, she had just been thinking that. At this rate it would hardly be worth her coming.

'Never mind. You'll have to put up with me instead.'

'Will you read me a story?'

Kate groaned. She was worrying now about the babysitter not being here and her patience was about to snap.

'I will,' Elinor stepped in with a smile. 'Now, you go and get into bed. I'll be up in a minute.'

'How is she?' Kate asked when Elinor came downstairs.

'A bit restless.'

'Not surprising with the amount of rubbish she's eaten.' Kate bit into a large slice of pizza. 'Enough to give an elephant stomach ache.'

As if on cue, the door opened.

'I can't sleep.'

'How do you know? You haven't tried yet.'

Emma scowled and rubbed a fist in her eye. 'There's something outside my room moving about.'

'No, there isn't,' Kate said, feeling her patience stretch again. 'Don't be silly.'

'There is!' Emma insisted. 'It's a ghost. The ghost who walks. He walks up and down the landing waiting to come into my room . . .'

Kate sighed, she'd heard Mum deal with this particular one before.

'There really isn't anyone there, Emma. It's just your

imagination. There's absolutely no reason at all to be frightened . . .'

'That's what Mum always says.' Emma shot her a look of withering contempt. She had expected better from someone near her own age.

'We'll leave the light on.'

'Mum says that, too.'

'Well, what do you want?'

'To stay down here with you.'

'No!' they all said together.

'Why not!' Emma wailed. 'It's not fair! I'm the only one on my own! You can all stay together. Even when you go to bed, Ellie's in with Kate, and Tom and Davey are sharing, I'll be all on my own. With the ghost . . .'

'There's nothing there!' Kate insisted. 'I just told you!'

'Not on the landing. Not that one. There's another one. There's two of them. There's one outside, scrabbling on the roof . . .'

'It's just the wind blowing the branches against the kitchen window.' Kate glared at her sister. 'You're just making a stupid fuss, trying to take advantage because Mum and Dad aren't here.'

'I'm not Katie, I'm not . . .' Emma's mouth wavered, near to genuine tears.

'Just go to bed!'

'All right,' Emma knew when the battle was lost. She straightened her small frame, and the top of her fleecy primrose pyjamas. She threw back her long fair hair in a passable imitation of her big sister, and fixed her with the same blue-eyed stare. They were quite similar in many ways and these clashes were not uncommon. 'All right, I'll go. But I'm telling Mum that you were nasty to me. Then you'll be sorry!'

Emma marched off, stamping her way up the stairs and across the landing, every step distinct.

'Let's all calm down.' Tom said as the bedroom door slammed. 'Shall we watch the video now? OK. Lights out . . .'

Davey stood up. 'Before we do that, there's something I've been wanting to talk about.'

'Like what?' Kate asked. 'If we leave it too long, Mum and Dad will be back before the end.'

'I've got a weird feeling . . .'

'Not *again*!' Kate rolled her eyes up to the ceiling. 'You and your weird feelings – you're worse than Emma! Come on, Tom. Let's watch the video.'

'Wait,' Elinor took the remote control out of her brother's reach. 'I want to hear what Davey has to say.'

'OK,' Kate sighed and stared at her brother.

'Well, er, it's kind of . . . Well, I'm not sure, really . . .' Davey blushed. With everyone's attention swinging his way, he couldn't think where to begin or what to say. 'It's just that tonight *is* Hallowe'en and I think we should be careful . . .'

'*Why*, for God's sake,' Tom shook his head. 'It's just a bit of fun.'

'It's hard to explain . . .' Davey took a deep breath. 'Well, it's about Derry House. Something happened in there. That's why . . . that's why I think we ought to be careful.'

He had their attention now all right. The remote control lay forgotten. Kate put her pizza down and Elinor sat forward, chin on hand, green eyes wide as Davey told his story.

'I think they're a ghost crew,' he concluded. 'And that's why we should be careful.'

'What do you mean?' Kate frowned. 'A *ghost crew*? I don't know what you're talking about . . .'

Davey shook his head impatiently. 'Yes, you do. At midsummer, when Tom and Ellie came for their birthdays, we went on the Ghost Walk, the Haunts Ghost Tour.'

'What?' Kate stared at him. 'You didn't want to go, as I recall. I thought we went for a pizza . . .'

'I know,' Davey looked at his sister. 'So did I, to start with, at least. But I had an odd feeling about that whole evening, like there was a chunk of time missing. Not on the clock,' he said quickly before any of them objected. 'In here,' he tapped the side of his head. 'Inside me. Then all these memories started coming up between what I *thought* had happened, and the two things didn't fit.'

'How do you mean?' Tom asked, intrigued.

'I'm not sure exactly,' Davey frowned, 'but I have memories, at least they feel like memories of incidents I can't quite locate. It started as dreams . . .'

'I've been having dreams,' Elinor said quietly. 'They began around that time. Dreams about people I don't know in real life.'

'Everyone has those,' Tom objected.

'Yes, but in the dream I *do* know them. Who they are and everything. There's a man: tall, dark, a bit younger than Dad. He's dressed as a pirate or something, or . . .'

'A highwayman?'

'Yes!' Elinor turned to Davey in surprise. 'How did you know?'

'I just do.'

'There's others, too,' Elinor supplied. 'A woman in a headscarf, and a girl with long, dark hair and a young boy. They wear old-fashioned clothes, but from different times. Sometimes I can hear music, a pipe and a violin, sometimes the dream is nice, friendly,' she hugged herself, then shuddered. 'Sometimes it is very scary.' She looked at the others, they had gone very quiet. 'What's the matter?'

'I have the same dreams,' Tom said after a while.

'Me, too,' Kate admitted, looking at her brother. 'And they scare me. What are we going to do?'

'Nothing,' Davey shrugged. 'If we sit tight, we should be OK. It's just—'

'Not a good time to watch *Halloween*?' Tom supplied.

'Exactly,' Davey smiled. 'It might bring those bad things into the house.' He looked around. 'Does that sound silly?'

'No,' Kate shook her head, 'not silly at all. You lot

178

decide what you want to do. I'd better go and check on Emma.'

'Davey? Can you come up here a minute?'

Kate's voice came down from upstairs. She was trying to sound normal, but there was a brittle edge of panic in her voice. They were out of their seats and up the stairs in an instant.

'What's the matter?' Davey gasped as he got to the door of Emma's room.

He did not have to look in to know. Kate's expression told it all: her face was chalk-white, her eyes wide, unblinking, as if she could not believe what she was seeing. Davey stared, too, his own eyes raking the room as terrible fear welled up inside him. He remembered his feeling about inviting in something bad. It was too late for that. It looked like somebody already had. Emma's bed was empty, the duvet smoothed down, everything neat and tidy. There was no sign that his little sister had even been in the room. Except for the red balloon. It seemed to look over at him, its clown mouth stretched in an evil grin as it bobbed up and down on the window sill, cross-patch eyes squeezed shut with mirth, its heavy head bent as if in silent laughter.

7

'She's probably hiding someplace,' Tom said. 'No need to panic.'

'Yeah,' his sister agreed. 'She was pretty cross at being left out. She's probably done it to teach us a lesson.'

'What if she isn't?' Kate looked round the small bedroom, at the little bed, the miniature desk and chair. Emma's cuddly toys stared back reproachfully. 'What if . . .'

'We'll search the house first,' Elinor squeezed her hand. 'Come on, let's get started.'

They looked everywhere. In every room, upstairs and down. Under beds, in wardrobes, in cupboards, even under the stairs. There was no sign of her.

'We'll have to call Mum and Dad,' Kate's hand trembled as she reached for the pad next to the phone in the hall. 'They'll go ballistic.'

The top page was blank. Kate blinked, unable to believe it. She had seen Mum write down the number of the place where they would be with her own eyes. She riffled through the rest of the pages, going backwards and forwards through the pad. Nothing. Every page was empty.

'Brilliant! Oh, that's brilliant!' She sank down on to a

chair, head in her hands. 'What are we going to do now?'

'Maybe Emma went outside,' Tom suggested.

'Why would she do that?'

'I don't know,' Tom shrugged. 'Like Ellie said, she was pretty annoyed.'

Kate shook her head, wiping away tears of panic with the back of her hand.

'Even Emma wouldn't do that. We have to call the police.'

'And tell them what? Your sister's been missing ten minutes? They'll probably think it's a hoax call. I bet they get loads on Hallowe'en.'

'Anyway,' Davey said quietly. 'They'll want to know where Mum and Dad are and we don't know, and we're here alone. We might get them into trouble.'

'Why don't we go out and take a quick look round?' Tom said. 'Just in case she slipped out for a prank. And then, if we haven't found her, say in half an hour, we'll call the cops. How about that?'

'One thing I don't understand,' Elinor frowned. 'How did she get out? All the doors are locked . . .'

'I don't know,' Davey replied. That had been bothering him, too.

He glanced about, confused, then he saw the dish of sweets left out for trick-or-treat. It was nearly empty. He remembered the flattened chocolates at the end of their drive. What if Mum had asked someone in to help themselves . . .

Davey had read somewhere that vampires had to be invited in before they could enter a house, but once over the threshold, they could come back any time they liked. Maybe what applied to one, applied to all, any evil spirit abroad . . .

That ghost crew, the clown and the other two, must have been to their house. They must have come back, but what would they want with Emma? He suddenly remembered the Fairy Raid, the Old Grey Man's daughter, with her pale hair and silver slanting eyes. He could see her now, riding on her horse, holding the little human boy she had stolen to be her toy . . .

He knew at that moment, just as surely as if he had been told, that if they left it to the police, or any normal agency, they would never see Emma again.

'I don't know,' he said again. 'But we have to go and find her.'

They decided to split the search. Davey would take his bike and go in wide sweeps, while the others would stick to the nearby streets.

Davey's mountain bike was newish, with lots of gears. He had been given it as a combined Christmas and birthday present the year before and had been careful to look after it. It was kept in the utility room at the back of the house behind the kitchen and he went round there now to get it out. As he opened the door, he glanced up. The utility room was little more than a lean-to. The low roof sloped up to the kitchen and from there it was a clear run up to Emma's room. Her window was very slightly ajar. They had not noticed that before because the curtains were drawn. He looked around on the ground. There were no foot marks that he could see, but then there wouldn't be.

Davey got his bike and met Tom and Elinor at the top of the drive. Kate was still inside the house trying to find Mum's address book. While they waited for her, Davey pointed out the squashed sweets.

'So, let me get this straight,' Tom said. 'You think the ones who took the sweets came back for Emma?'

Davey nodded. 'I think they're the same ones that lured me into Derry House.'

'And you reckon they're a ghost crew?'

Davey nodded again. 'Yes. It's the same as on the Ghost Walk, but in reverse. Last time we went into their world, in the city. This time they've come into ours.'

'Kind of like ghost 'burbs?' Tom folded his arms and grinned. He always wanted to make a joke of things. 'I see what you mean.'

Although the evening had been quite mild earlier, it was getting cold now. Kate shivered as she joined them, pulling her coat closer as Davey explained his theory.

'I'm not sure . . .' she said when he had finished. This kind of talk could be wasting time, distracting them from the real issue which was finding Emma. 'Who are we supposed to be looking for?'

'This ghost crew! The leader's wearing a dirty white tunic with a cross on it, he's in a kind of death mask, greeny white – that's if it is a mask. He's got a monk with him, hood up over a skeleton face. And there's a clown dressed in red, with a white face and crimson wig, like Pennywise, the clown in that Stephen King film.'

'Maybe they were just people dressed up. There are plenty out in fancy dress, maybe they were just playing a trick on you. You don't know for sure they were a ghost crew . . .'

'They are, Kate. Honestly, you've got to believe me.'

'We just can't risk it, Davey,' Kate looked at her brother. 'We can't waste time on what might turn out to be a wild goose chase. The night is cold, Emma's out in her pyjamas, as far as we know, and she could freeze to death.' She paused. 'I don't think we can handle this by ourselves. It was stupid to think we could in the first place. I'm going to the police station. You can come with me if you like but I'm going anyway. I can't see any alternative.'

'I think you're right,' Tom agreed.

'Me too.' Elinor moved in beside Kate.

Davey didn't move. He knew that, in one way, the ordinary way, his sister was right. But he also knew that this was not an ordinary night. He knew that what Kate wanted was the sensible thing to do, the only thing to do in normal circumstances. But these were not normal circumstances. There was a sinister crew about. They had lured him into Derry House. Then there was the way the food had changed at the disco, turning to something disgusting . . .

There was definitely something weird happening and Emma's disappearance was connected with it, he was certain.

'But there *is* something going on here,' he pleaded. 'Can't you feel it, too?'

Elinor shrugged. 'Can't say I do.'

Her brother shook his head. 'Me, neither.'

'Well there is,' Davey insisted. 'You've got to listen—'

'I just think we're wasting time.' Kate had made up her mind. 'I'm going to the police.'

'Wait! Kate!'

Kate shook her head, denying Davey's pleading. She was responsible. She was the eldest. It was time to think like an adult would do. She was in charge after all, particularly since Zoe had never showed up. That was another strange thing . . . but there was probably a perfectly simple explanation for that.

She thrust her hands in her pockets and went to step on to the path when Tom pulled her back.

'Hang on a minute, Kate,' he whispered. 'Look down there. Maybe Davey's got something.'

Further down the rise, a figure was emerging from one of the narrow entries that ran beside some of the houses. He came out at a crouch, dirty white gown touching the ground. There was something sneaky – furtive – in the way he crept out and looked up and down the deserted road, his white rubber mask face twisting this way and that. When he was sure there was no one about he gestured forward, urging others to come out.

They emerged one at a time. First the dark-robed skeleton, his skull face luminous under the street light, scanning the road with empty socket eyes, and finally the clown. A flash of colour after white and black: red hair, white face, red baggy costume, with a swathe of yellow . . .

'It's them.' Davey leaned out from the hedge, risking a better look. 'Now do you believe me—' The clown was carrying something. 'What's that? Looks like a cloak, or a big tote bag . . .'

Davey pointed silently, urging the others to see what lay draped over the clown's shoulder. Arms hung down. Blonde hair fell into folds of red silk. It was Emma.

8

The crew were crossing the road one at a time, heading for the alleyway that led between the houses on the opposite side.

'What are we going to do?' Kate whispered, trying to keep her panic down.

'We can't take them all on,' Davey said. 'I'll go down on my bike, try to head the first two off. You follow the clown.'

'Where do you think he's taking her?' Tom whispered.

'We can't know for certain,' Davey replied, 'but my guess is Derry House.'

He was up on his bike and away before the others could stop him. The lead two of the ghost crew were already on the other side of the road, some way ahead of the clown who, encumbered by his burden, was making slower progress.

'OK,' Davey yelled as he got near, 'you want me – come and get me!'

The klansman and the skeleton leapt out of the way, scattering towards the alley as the bike closed in on them.

The suddenness of Davey's attack surprised the clown, catching him in the middle of the road. He stopped and looked around, as if unsure what to do. He clearly did not like being out in the open like this, exposed for anyone to see. He hesitated for a moment and then retreated, retracing his steps, seeking the shelter of the entry from which he had just emerged.

A mass of short-cuts and walkways, garages and parking bays, lay at the back of the houses. The clown was likely to keep to those rather than risk being seen back on the main roads. Kate led Tom and Elinor down the side of next door's garden. She knew the hidden ways of the estate like the back of her hand.

They worked their way across, hoping to intercept the clown on his way down to Derry House. At first there was no sign of him. Then Tom caught a flash of colour between the parked cars.

He grabbed Kate's arm.

'I thought I saw something,' he whispered.

'Where?'

'Over there . . .'

Tom led the way as they dodged round the edge of the garages, inching to the corner, keeping close to the doors. He gestured for the others to move up.

'I don't see him.' Kate peered round.

Elinor looked at the deserted tarmac space in front of them. There were three ways in and out. The way they had come, the one where Katie was looking now, the vehicle access into the street, and a narrow pathway with brambles growing through broken chainlink fencing.

'Perhaps he went that way.' She pointed.

'No,' Kate shook her head. 'It's a dead end . . .'

There was a scuffle from the narrow path.

'Back!' Tom grabbed his sister and cousin and pushed them in between tall green wheelie bins. 'He's coming back! It's him. It's the clown!'

The words were scarcely out of his mouth when the clown came into view. He emerged from the narrow footpath, pulling bramble branches from his scarlet satin suit. Tufts of bright red hair streamed back from the bulging bald forehead of the grotesque white mask covering his face. Thin lines swept up and looped around little gleaming eyes set deep either side of the bulbous red nose. He stopped at the point where the path entered the area and paused to look round furtively, assessing the space before him. It had been getting colder, frost glistened on the ground in front of his big clown boots.

Kate had never been so terrified. She watched, wide-eyed like a hypnotised rabbit, as his heavy head swung slowly from side to side, his big sticking-out ears trying to pick up the slightest sound. She was sure he sensed that they were there. She held her breath, afraid that the rasp of air from her chest would give them away. Her heart was beating loud, thudding painfully against her ribs, surely he *must* hear that? Kate felt Elinor trembling next to her. She was feeling it badly, too. Some creatures can smell fear. The clown lifted his head suddenly and began snuffling, as if he was scenting, questing for them, ready to home in on their hiding place.

He stood, big head forward, his body bent and crouched, his hand and arm circling the yellow burden on his shoulder in a protective, cradling gesture. He carried the bundle as if it weighed nothing.

His eyes, liquid and black in the stark white face, flicked back and forth over the area and lighted on the wheelie bins. His thick red lips wrinkled back in a snarl to show yellow teeth, sharp inside the wide clown smile . . .

9

It had worked! The skeleton and the klansman were running away, fleeing before him! Davey felt heady with victory. Elated by the success of his shock attack, he changed into his fastest gear and stood on the pedals. He was flying like the wind now and he intended to run them down. That would pay them back for trying to frighten him and daring to take his sister. There could be no escape.

Except there was. One minute they were there in front of him, the next they had disappeared. Davey rode around until his legs ached, up and down street after street, into the village and down to the Hollow, and still he could find no sign of them. He was tiring now. His legs were really hurting. The ghost crew seemed to have vanished into the air. He found himself free-wheeling downhill, back towards the Hollow. The bike seemed to be riding itself . . .

Davey had not really meant to come this way. He snapped out of his drifting fatigue to find himself at the top of the drive leading down to Derry House. He tried to bring the bike to a halt, but found himself peddling instead, his wheels jolting and bumping over the uneven surface of the buckled tarmac.

Behind him came the squeal of metal on metal, the grating protest of rusting hinges, long disused, being forced into action. Davey stopped his bike and looked back to see the big wooden gates swinging shut behind him. The klansman stood in front of them, brawny arms folded, grinning down towards him. Davey looked wildly round and saw the skeleton man sneaking out of the shadows. Derry House was the end of a cul-de-sac. Davey's hands froze on the handlebars. They had him trapped.

Unless . . .

There was one chance, and slim at that. Davey adjusted his front light and stamped on the pedals, adrenalin pumping his legs. The skeleton thing made a snatch for him, causing Davey to wobble dangerously but he was going downhill. He managed to keep the front wheel straight and built up speed quickly, but the thing kept pace with him, moving silently, effortlessly, a skeletal hand came out, grabbing for him, Davey felt the bone digging in, scraping his skin.

'Get off me!' he roared and veered the bike away.

The other one, the klansman, was coming after him now, shadowing his other side, trying to out-flank him. Davey swerved away from hands as big as goalkeeper's gloves, if that thing grabbed him, he'd stay grabbed.

They were nearing the back of the house, only metres away stood a solid wall of evergreen bushes. Except it was not as solid as it looked. Generations of children had cut through Derry Hollow on their way to school. There were gaps easily wide enough to take a boy and a bike. Davey had been that way lots of times, although not in the dark, and certainly not at night. Sending up a quick prayer, he crouched down low and aimed the bike.

'What was that? Sounded like Davey.'

Kate and Tom heard it at the same time and both turned their heads.

The clown had heard it, too. He looked up and away as if he was being called. He stood for a moment with his head on one side, listening, and then he tightened his grip on Emma. He loped away, hardly glancing at the place where they were hiding, as if he had better things to do.

'Quick! Come on!' Tom beckoned the other two out. 'We have to follow him, find out where he's taking her.'

'What are we going to do when we catch up with him?' Elinor asked as they padded along the footpath.

'I don't know,' her brother shrugged. 'It depends . . .'

'On what?'

'Where he's heading and where the other two are. The ones Davey went after.' Tom frowned, and looked around. 'We don't know what's happened to them and we don't want to be ambushed. We'll just have to keep a good look out for them as well.'

There was no sign of the rest of the crew, or Davey. He seemed to have succeeded in keeping them out of the way. The clown took a zig-zag path through the estate, keeping to entries and back alleys. The children tracked him, careful not to be seen. It was not difficult to work out where he was heading. All the time they were moving downwards – into Derry Hollow.

Kate, Tom and Elinor stayed as close as they dared, but the clown seemed to melt into the darkness surrounding the place. They thought they had lost him, then they caught a flash of red flitting across the car park, disappearing round the side of the house, going towards the back.

'What are we going to do now?' Elinor whispered to Kate.

'Follow him in.'

'Aren't you frightened?'

Kate looked up at the big old house with its jutting roofs and empty windows. It had been scary enough before, now it seemed even more terrifying. A milky-white fog was creeping up, lapping at the bottom storey. All around was darkness. The house seemed to be floating in a different world, on a sea made up of mist and shadows.

'Of course I'm frightened!'

Kate was so scared her whole body was shaking, but she would face whatever was in there. She would do anything to save Emma.

'Come on, let's go.' Tom motioned them forward and they slipped over the gate and across the car park, as silent as phantoms, disappearing one after another into the rapidly rising fog.

10

Davey made it through the hedge. He held himself steady for the metre-high drop on the other side and hit the ground with a teeth rattling thump. He did not bother to check whether he was being followed, but rode straight across the field, over Gilmore Bridge, up Shaker's Lane and on to the Heath beyond.

Wesson Heath had once covered a great area, spreading wild and open for many miles, merging into the King's Wood, one of the great hunting forests which in turn had extended far to the south. In those days it had been a dangerous place, with a bad reputation for lawlessness. Now there were only patches of genuine heathland left. Modern development had nibbled the rest away, shrinking the wilderness to a few square miles, but it still had its own atmosphere. The land either side of the road was unfenced, uncultivated. There were no hedges and the few trees were bent and gnarled by the wind.

Davey thought for a while that he had got clean away. He slackened off his pace and stopped his bike, ready to go back. When he turned, his whole body froze. They were after him. Across the featureless landscape, he could see a figure all dressed in white, flapping along like some joke shop ghost. Next to it, a skull gleamed fluorescent in the darkness.

He jumped back on his bike, but his legs felt like lead weights welded to the pedals as he stood in his saddle to negotiate Whitestone Hill. The Whitestone, a dirty quartz boulder, still lay at the crossroads at the top. The stone, a marker of some kind, had been there from time out of mind. On its surface, a faded arrow pointed to the city, numbers underneath noting the distance, but the stone had been there long before man measured his journeys in miles. No one was quite sure of its original purpose, but it had been placed there deliberately. No rock of that type occurred locally.

The stone marked a place of some importance: where four roads met. In times gone by this would have been the meeting place of witches and warlocks, or so it is said. A gibbet had swung there, creaking out a warning to felons and wrongdoers, until almost within living memory.

Whitestone Hill was the highest point on Wesson Heath. High and windswept, it had always been a lonely spot, and still was. A large roundabout had replaced the crossroads and a modern bypass swept around the rough tongue of land. The old roads were narrow, with broken verges and pot-holed surfaces. No one came here much, except to fly kites and walk dogs.

The night was clear and cold. Stars glittered like frost round a new moon as thin as a fingernail. Davey reached the top of the hill and stopped. His front wheel skidded from underneath him. There was frost on the ground as well. He did not really know why he had come up here. The ground was open, bare of cover. It was not a good place to hide.

He left his bike where it lay and went over to the crossroads. An old wooden signpost showed the way from one place to another. Davey sank down on his knees beside it. He no longer cared if the ghost crew followed him up here. He bowed his head, leaning forward until his hands were resting on the cold rough surface of the Whitestone, its crystal facets shining like ice in the moonlight. He could go no further.

Once you have tried the possible, there is only the impossible left.

He remembered reading that somewhere. He let out a call, a cry for help to whoever, whatever, might be there, but no one was listening. His vision blurred and cleared as he blinked back tears. He was too tired to escape. All he could do was stay and wait for them to come and get him. His only hope, his only comfort was that he might have acted as a decoy, allowing the others to rescue Emma, but even that was far from certain. Eventually he stopped fighting the tears and let them flow down his face. What did it matter? There was no one up here to see him cry.

He did not know what length of time had passed. It could have been minutes, or it could have been hours. A noise, a sound on the road. Not footsteps padding at a steady pace, coming to hunt him down, but an altogether different sound: horse's hooves, beating on the metalled surface and they were coming nearer.

'Who calls me here?' The rider's voice was cold, stern in the surrounding silence.

The horse came to a halt before him and Davey looked up, wiping his face with his sleeve. The animal stood huge, chest heaving, great legs trembling. Sweat showed on its black neck. It snorted, breathing hard, mane shining in silver ripples as it shook its head and pawed the ground. It had been ridden fast and the night was freezing, but no white puffs of air showed at its nostrils.

'I repeat,' the rider was dismounting, swinging himself out of the saddle. 'Who calls me here?'

Davey scrambled to his feet. The man held the bridle in one gloved hand, the other rested on the pommel of his short sword. His thigh boots were splashed and spattered and there was mud on the bottom of his velvet coat. A cocked hat curling with feathers shaded a face half covered by a black mask. He wore a scarf loosely looped round his neck and looked like a guest on route to a fancy dress party, but Davey knew that these were the clothes that he always wore, they belonged to his time.

'Is it Davey?' A smile split the fearsome face. 'Jack Cade, at your service.' He removed his hat and mask and bowed down. 'I had not thought to see you again.'

'Same here.' Davey smiled shyly. The highwayman

looked younger, friendlier, without his hat and mask, altogether not so imposing,

Davey blinked, unable to quite believe his eyes. Jack Cade, the highwayman, had ridden straight out of his dreams. He had come straight out of that strange interlude at midsummer and was standing here now, large as life.

'But I don't understand,' Davey managed to say. 'I – I thought you kept to your own areas. What are you doing here – out of the city?'

'The Heath is one of my haunts,' the highwayman answered. 'In life I was often here about my business.'

'Robbing coaches?'

The highwayman laughed, 'And horsemen. Anyone who came along.'

'Why are you here now, though?' Davey asked.

'Because you called me,' Jack Cade answered simply. 'You saved me from the Judge's gallows. I am in your debt. But tell me, young Davey. Why are *you* here, with your face besmirched and dressed so strangely, on this night of all nights, when all manner of evil is about.'

Davey touched his face. It was still streaked with Terror of the Crypt paint and he was wearing the grave suit under his coat.

'It's Hallowe'en,' he mumbled.

'I know that!'

'We dress as ghosts and go begging for sweets.'

'I see,' the highwayman's heavy black eyebrows lifted and the corner of his mouth twitched. 'It was not the custom in my day, but times change. But you have not answered my question. What are you doing up on the heath on the Eve of All Hallows?'

'There's a ghost crew loose in the village. I was trying to get away from them – they've taken my sister—'

'Mistress Kate?' Jack Cade's dark brows contracted in alarm.

'No,' Davey shook his head. 'I have another one. A little one. Emma. She's wasn't with us on the ghost walk. She was too small to go. She's only eight—'

Davey broke off trying to control a sudden surge of feeling which caused fresh tears to block his throat.

'You come from the village yonder,' Jack said after a while, nodding towards the lights below them.

'Yes.'

'Hmm. It has long been a place of evil reputation.'

'It's quite respectable now,' Davey objected, slightly stung by the implication.

'That's as maybe,' the highwayman smiled. 'But if that is so, why do you require my help, young Davey? Do you know the *Plume of Feathers*?'

'Yes,' Davey nodded. 'It's a pub in the village, at the top of Shaker's Lane. It's called the *Firkin* something.'

'Ever a haunt of evil-doers. A parcel of rogues and vagabonds, gaming men and gamblers, the rough element from the city come to wager on prize fighting, cock fighting, bull baiting. A den of robbers, thieves, and worse. Some say that's why they have the gibbet hereabouts. To save the magistrates the expense of sending them to the city to be hanged.'

Jack looked up at the signpost. Above his head, Davey thought he heard something creak

'I don't see . . .' Davey frowned, not sure what Jack was talking about.

'We have a saying in the city, "*a place cannot change its ghosts*". Tonight is Hallowe'en. A night when ghosts walk and spirits are abroad. Here too, in your village, the same as everywhere else.' He paused. 'There are those who do not wish you well. When you were in the city you made powerful enemies.'

'Who? The Judge?'

'No,' Jack laughed, hard and hollow. 'Worse. Much worse. Don't you remember the Old Grey Man's daughter?'

Davey remembered all right. He felt his insides congeal with fear.

'Do you think she's after me?'

'Not just you.'

'Emma!' Davey nodded, he had already thought that might be so.

The highwayman inclined his head. 'The Lady is much displeased with you, and she's not a one to let things lie. She has likely bribed a ghost crew from the pack of rogues I described. She would not risk her father's wrath by using her own people. He is not as fond as she is of meddling in your world. She is much more likely to use ghosts to seize your sister and deliver her.'

'But why?'

'She belongs to an ancient and savage breed. They live by the old beliefs: an eye for an eye, a child for a child.'

'Oh, no,' Davey grabbed his bike again. 'Not because of me. That's not fair. To take her for something *I've* done . . .'

'Wait. Wait!' Jack Cade held his arm. 'Where are you going?'

'To find her.'

'On your own? You do not stand a chance.'

'That may be so,' Davey shook his head, tears threatening again. 'But it's better than just standing here talking. I have to go.'

'Not alone. I will come with you.' He tightened his grip on Davey's arm. 'We will find her together.'

'There is something awry here.'

The highwayman reined the horse in and stopped. Davey looked over his shoulder to the village which lay strung out before them, ranged down the side of the opposite hill. Mist was pouring out of the Hollow, stealing up the slope, spreading out like dry ice all along the low-lying ground.

'It's natural,' Davey remarked. 'You often get fog this time of year, especially down there.'

'There is nothing natural about this,' the highwayman's brow creased in a grim frown. 'It is eldritch.'

203

He muttered the word as though unwilling to speak it aloud.

'What does that mean?'

'Uncanny. Fey, faerie. I sense the Sidhe, the Unseelie Court.'

'What, all of them?'

Davey's eyes widened as he recalled the Fairy Raid. Hundreds had paraded past then. Some were big, others small; some hideously ugly, others beautiful beyond recall. They had gone by as he'd lain hidden. He remembered praying that they would never, never see him. Their unhuman strangeness had made his blood run cold.

'No, I think not all,' Jack Cade stared down at the village, his face thoughtful. 'Although Dwerry Hollow is one of their places. I think the Lady comes alone on business of her own, as I said.'

He turned on his saddle and whistled through his white teeth, a single note, sharp and piercing.

'Who are you calling?'

'One who may be of assistance.'

'The Blind Fiddler?'

'Alas, no. He is busy in the city. Nor can Polly, Elizabeth or Govan aid us. This is not their place. The one I call was here long before me. Once, in life, I did him a service. Now we haunt the place together. Before the night is out, we may need him. Do not be afraid of him.' The highwayman turned and looked down at Davey perched behind his saddle. 'But, if you are, do not show your fear.'

Jack Cade spurred his horse on. Nobody joined them. Davey was beginning to think that Jack had sent his call out for nothing when, quite suddenly, he became aware of another presence. There was something alongside them. Davey looked down and almost immediately wished that he had not. His arms went rigid, he nearly lost his grip around the horseman's waist and felt himself slipping. Trotting along beside them was an enormous dog. It was black, like a labrador, but with long shaggy fur. Wide across the shoulder and back, thick set like a rottweiler, but much, much bigger. It was more like a newfoundland, or an Irish wolfhound but even breeds of that size would have looked puny next to this creature. It was up to the horse's flank. The animal's thick black fur seemed frosted in blue-white light, haloed in static. Davey tucked his leg as far up as possible, fearing that his foot might touch its back.

The creature did not look up. He stared straight on, his huge head swinging from side to side with his heavy loping gait. Drool dripped from his massive jaws, splashing shining green phosphorescence, and his eyes lit the ground in front of him like twin red headlights.

'What is that!' Davey had never seen anything like it. He had no idea that a thing like this even existed. His voice came out squeaky with terror. He drew his legs up even further, until they were nearly under his chin, and clung on very tight to Jack's back.

'He goes under many names,' the highwayman replied. 'Black Dog, Barguest, Skriker – Guytrash. He is the object of great dread. A beast of ill omen. In the ordinary way of things, it is death to even look at him.' He felt Davey tense behind him. 'But do not worry,' he added, quick to reassure the boy. 'He will do you no harm. While you are with me you are safe.'

Davey believed him, but just to be sure, he turned his head to the other side, closed his eyes and kept them shut all the way to the Hollow.

11

'Which way did they go?' Kate looked around at a loss.

Elinor shrugged, 'I don't know.'

They had rounded the first corner, moving towards the back of Derry House. Emma and the clown figure had seemed only seconds in front, but now there was no sign of them. The fog was thickening fast.

'We must have missed them.' Kate turned to go back. 'Maybe they went in at the front. Maybe they doubled back without us noticing.'

'It's no good just running around in a panic.' Tom held her arm. 'They came this way definitely and we weren't that far behind them. They can't have got past us. Leastways, *I* didn't see them.' He turned to his sister. 'Did you?'

Elinor shook her head.

'The best thing to do is start a systematic search.'

'But what are we looking for?' Kate was desperate with anxiety. It could take all night.

'Another way in for a start off.'

Tom looked around, assessing the area. The tarmac was marked with parking bays. A row of bins stood under high windows which were all closed. He went up some steps and tried a side door but it was locked tight, bolted from the inside. To the left was a grating. A flash of his torch showed a thick layer of leaves and litter beneath a smeary, dirt-encrusted basement window. There was no way of getting down there, though. The rusty metal bars were set in concrete.

Next to the grating more bins stood against the wall of the house. Tom walked round them. They were big galvanised wheelies, much taller than him. The last one stuck out from the others at a forty-five degree angle. Tom knelt down, using his torch again. Reefs of dirt and a semicircle of bleached grass showed that the bin had only recently been moved out of position. He flashed the beam around the immediate area and picked up the gleam of metal. He backed away, surveying the area carefully. The bin had been half on a trap door maybe two metres across.

'Come here.' He beckoned the others over. 'Take a look at this.'

'What?' Kate looked over his shoulder.

'It's some kind of trap door. For delivering things straight into the cellar.'

He reached forward. The iron doors met in the middle and were opened by means of rings countersunk into their edges. He pulled one experimentally. It came up quite easily.

'Shine the torch over here, Tom.' His sister pulled his arm. 'Under the bin. There's something under the wheels.'

Tom went over to investigate. The wheels were like giant rollerskates. He reached under, but the object was trapped.

He stood up. 'We'll have to shift it. Give us a hand, Kate.'

The two put their shoulders to the bin. It was empty and moved easily. Elinor leaned in to retrieve the thing she'd seen and held it up to Kate.

Kate took it from her, turning it over as fog wreathed like smoke in the torch beam. It was one of Emma's cat slippers. She'd got them last Christmas. They were getting a bit too small for her now, but Emma wouldn't hear of getting new ones. They were blue, going through at the toe, with a red pom-pom nose and black whiskers.

'It's hers. Definitely.' Kate could hardly breathe. 'They must have gone down . . .'

'You take that side, I'll take this.' Tom directed his sister to seize the ring in the other trap door. 'And quietly! What ever you do, don't let it clang . . .

The doors were very heavy. Kate helped Elinor and the two of them lowered their half slowly and gently. The other side was too much for Tom on his own. It would have taxed the strength of a grown man. The metal was bitingly cold and the fog had covered everything with a film of moisture. The ring slipped from his hand. The noise of iron on concrete was enough to wake the entire neighbourhood. Jack spurred on as, across the heath, he and Davey heard the bang.

'Oh, well . . . Can't be helped . . .'

Tom was shaking, but he had to put a brave face on it. There was a shriek from within and it sounded distinctly human. They couldn't back out now, not with Emma so near. Their only hope was that the sudden noise had brought an element of confusion. Perhaps they could take advantage of that to spring a surprise attack.

The trap door opened above a flight of steps. Tom led the way down. There was no one in the first room, but an archway in the thick stone walls opened into another larger area.

The Lady was not hard to find. The Old Grey Man's daughter wasn't trying to hide. She was in the largest room in the basement. It ran under the entire back of the house and had once been used as a laundry room. Faint light from outside filtered through long, sloping, rusty framed windows of dirty pebbled glass. A line of old-fashioned sinks stood under these and drying racks hung from the ceiling. The opposite wall held the pipes for plumbed-in washing machines.

In the centre of the room, standing absolutely still, was the Wicked Queen from *Snow White*, or rather what Kate had always imagined her to look like. A tall cloaked figure wearing a long gown, in her black hair she wore a golden crown. Kate saw her as the Queen had appeared when she'd looked into her mirror. Her lips, crimson against her creamy skin, curled in a secret smile. Her thin brows arched above black eyes half closed, sleepy with evil, full of adult guile, as she scanned the magic surface, searching for poor Snow White.

Elinor stared transfixed with terror at what she thought to be the Grand High Witch from *The Witches* by Roald Dahl. She had never confessed this to anyone, but as a small child this particular character had petrified her. Grandma had read the story to her and Tom. He had chuckled and laughed, while she had lain there, night after night, only seeing the vilest cruelty. These women kill children. Who couldn't see the hideous truth that lay behind their beauty?

Tom saw the Ice Queen, the White Witch from *The Lion, the Witch and the Wardrobe*. A tall lady dressed in furs with a crown on her head with red, red lips and skin as white as snow. She was beautiful, but distant and dangerous, like an arctic sunset. He saw her cold beauty and ached deep inside. He had always wanted to be her Prince and wear the gold crown and eat the Turkish Delight until he sickened, just like Edmund in the story.

All three stared at the woman in front of them, eyes wide and fixed, all seeing different things. The Old Grey Man's daughter. A mistress of disguise, the Lady could appear as anyone she liked. It pleased her now to show herself as the figure of dread who had stolen into their minds from the pages of childhood stories; to clothe herself in the very fabric of their deepest fears and leave them terrified.

Emma stood at her feet, eyes glazed, staring straight ahead, her face blank, free of all expression. The woman held her by the shoulder with one hand, while the other smoothed the child's pale silky hair.

That caress seemed to wake Kate from her trance.

'Let go of her!' she shouted.

The Lady just smiled and shook her head.

'I don't understand what you want with her!'

'Your brother sought to cheat me on Midsummer Eve of a child I had set my heart upon. So I will take your sister instead.'

Kate lunged forward, but the Lady froze her with a glance.

'Not so fast!' She laughed, a tinkling sound like icicles falling. 'Do you think I will give her up as easily as that?'

'What about you?' She turned to the others. 'Don't you want to save your little cousin?'

Tom and Elinor looked at Kate stuck in mid-stride, her arms stretched out, and back at the woman. Her gaze seemed to freeze and burn at the same time, like liquid nitrogen. Tom averted his eyes and bowed his head.

'I see you do not.' Her laughter was now heavy with mockery. 'You humans show such loyalty to kin and kind. Where is the other one?' Her tone changed, no longer mocking, it became thin and harsh like a rapier cutting through air. 'The boy, your cousin. Davey?'

'I – I don't know . . .' Tom stammered.

'Do not lie to me!' She was near now. She took his chin between cold fingers, forcing him to look at her. 'I will have your heart out! I will—'

'I – I'm not lying!' Tom twisted away, desperate to escape her terrible eyes, black and silver at the same time. 'I – I'd tell you if I could! Honest I would!'

'What about you?' She turned to Elinor. 'Do you know?'

Ellie looked back, pupils dilated with terror. 'No! No, I don't.' She shook her head and began to cry. 'We don't know anything!'

The fear and the tension were proving too much. Once Ellie started weeping, she could not stop. Her body was racked with sobs. Tears poured from her eyes, coursing down her cheeks. The Lady stepped away, anxious to avoid salt water. Human emotion disgusted her.

'I'll get it out of them, my Lady.' The clown stepped out of the shadows. Red lips in his white clown face parted in a grin, showing a black gap edged with jagged yellow teeth. 'You see if I don't.'

12

'I don't like this.'

Kate and Davey's mother stood listening to the dialling tone, biting her lip.

'I'm sure they're perfectly safe. They've probably gone to bed,' her husband said. 'For goodness' sake, Alison.'

Stephen Williams leaned against the wall in their host's hall, impatient to get back to the party. Everything had been going fine until his wife had decided to give the kids a ring. He had advised against it. They were bound to be all right and he did not want the evening spoilt by Alison worrying. They did not get out together very often and out of sight was out of mind as far as he was concerned.

'If they are in bed, why doesn't Zoe answer?' Alison Williams twisted the phone cord round her hand as the dialling tone droned on. 'She is supposed to be baby-sitting.'

Stephen shrugged. 'Maybe she's upstairs. Maybe she's got the TV on and her boyfriend's there . . .'

'I'm phoning Zoe's house.' Alison put the receiver down. 'I've got the number somewhere in my bag.'

'What on earth for?' Stephen took his hands out of his pockets and came over to her. 'I mean, what's the point?'

'My own peace of mind, that's what for. I have a bad feeling, it's been growing all evening . . .'

'Oh, no,' her husband groaned and rolled his eyes to the ceiling. 'Not one of your mum's premonitions!'

'You may mock, Stephen,' his wife said as she pored through her address book, 'but she's been right more times than she's been wrong. And before we left, Davey was behaving oddly. I've been worrying about him all evening. He could be going down with something. He was all jumpy and moody, not like himself at all . . . Ah, here it is – Zoe Vale, 937—' she began punching in the number.

'But Ali—'

'Hello, is that Mrs Vale? Alison Williams here. Sorry to disturb you so late, but—' she paused, listening to whatever Zoe's mother had to say. 'Has she?' Another pause, then, 'Did she? I see. Are you sure, sure it was . . . ? Oh, right, I see. You answered. Oh, no, no, there's no problem.' She turned away to face the wall. 'No, no, don't do that. Some kind of mix up. Yes. Exactly. Like I said, sorry to disturb you.'

Alison put the phone down slowly and stayed for a moment looking at the wallpaper in front of her. She did not have to say anything, Stephen knew something was wrong, badly wrong, as soon as she turned back to him.

'What's up, love?' He stepped forward, full of concern now, his previous annoyance forgotten. 'What's happened?'

'I don't know . . .' she shook her head. 'Mrs Vale said that Zoe has gone out with her boyfriend . . .'

'That's typical!' Her husband exploded. 'I *told* you she was too young! She's barely older than they are! You just can't rely on someone of that age!'

'She's seventeen,' his wife replied absently, 'and a sensible girl. We've never had any trouble with her before. Anyway, that's not the point. Her mum said the reason she'd gone out tonight was that I had phoned earlier—'

'You? Saying what?'

'That I didn't need her any more.'

They made their excuses and began their homeward journey, Alison driving, Stephen having had too much to drink. As soon as they were out of the drive, Alison noticed the first few ribbons of fog sliding across the glistening black tarmac. She turned the heating up and put the fog lights on, muttering a quick prayer under her breath, pleading for it not to be bad.

It seemed no one was there to answer her prayers.

The fog came on fast, thickening the air in front of the car, swirling in the headlights, surging up the wings like a sea of smoke. What had begun as white wisps rapidly turned to a blanket capable of enveloping everything. Alison had to change to a lower gear and slow the car to a crawl.

Fog would certainly lengthen the journey home. Once

off the bypass it was bound to be much worse. That road was low lying, down by the river, twisting and turning through one of the last tracts of ancient woodland hereabouts. Usually she loved to drive that way, day or night, it was a bit of true countryside, but tonight it was going to be a real nuisance. Still, it couldn't be helped. The other way involved a huge detour right around Wesson Heath. If they wanted to get home before morning, the Old Forest Road was the only route that they could take.

13

Despite Jack's words of reassurance, some kind of deep instinct told Davey not to look directly at the creature padding by his side. It might look like a dog but it was as big as a pony or a good sized calf, and then there were those eyes! Red light shone from them, lighting the night in front of him, staining the white mist pink.

'How do you know for certain that you can trust him?' Davey whispered, leaning forward.

'The Guytrash? He's a good friend. I once rendered him a service, as I told you.'

'What service?' Davey asked.

'In life, I used to work the Heath. It was much bigger then, a wild and lonely place, but coaches and travellers had to traverse it. The village where you live was the only settlement for miles around. It was a sorry place, much run down. Its people surly and secretive, not averse to a little robbery on their own account. It was one of their number who betrayed me . . .' he paused. 'But that's another story.'

'Did you rob anyone who came along?'

'Not the poor,' the highwayman laughed. 'But do not mistake me for Robin Hood, there is no point in stealing from those who have nothing. I took from the rich, those who had enough to spare and more – single horsemen or by the coachful. It was a good living. Anyway, one summer evening, just as night was falling, I was riding back to the city after a good day's work, back to my Polly at *The Seven Dials*. I was riding between two high banks when I heard a noise, somewhere between a growl and a whine, like a creature in pain; but unearthly, strange enough to chill the blood. I thought to spur on, the light was fading, night was coming, but my horse stopped dead in her tracks, nostrils flaring, ears back. She was whinnying, staring up at the hedgerow at the side of the deep defile. The groans were louder now, coming from the other side. Dell shied, it was all I could do to keep her from bolting. I dismounted and tied her to a tree, I did not want her to gallop off and leave me stranded.

'I found a gap in the hedge and climbing an old stile, I could see a dark shape lying up under the hawthorn. I thought at first that I had come across a pony or a calf, injured perhaps by dogs, and I had heard tell of wolves left up on the Chase from long ago. The noises the creature was making were like nothing that I had ever heard and, as I approached, I confess that thoughts of the Guytrash did cross my mind. I had heard tales of the fearsome creature said to haunt the Heath, but I had dismissed them as old wives' cant and superstition. But, when I ventured nearer, I had cause to change my opinion . . .

'The creature was lying down, twisted round, trying to lick his haunch. I could see now that he was a dog, but of

219

marvellous size. He was a magnificent creature, none-theless, and I said as much as I came near. I have ever liked dogs, and they in general like me, so although he gave a deep-throated growl, his heart wasn't in it. He was nearly spent, I don't know how far he'd run on that wounded leg, for wounded it was. Blood glistened black on his coat, running down to a pool on the ground.

'I said; "Good dog, good boy," or some such, but in truth I was terrified. By now I knew well who he was, and it is death to see the Guytrash. He looked up, his great eyes dimmed, their red fire nearly gone. I was shaking with fear but I couldn't leave him in pain. I had come this far, I could not turn away. For any animal, I would do the same.'

'What did you do?'

'I knelt beside him to look at his leg, talking soothing nonsense all the while, just as though he was a normal dog. There was an elf bolt buried up to the flight. The flesh was swollen round it, the wound was festering and bleeding afresh from where he had been worrying at it. He would die without help, I had no doubt. Maybe he knew it too, because he made no move even though my touch must have pained him. If it was to be done, it was best done quickly. So I took what I could find of the shaft and pulled with all my might. The pain must have been cruel, but the only sound he made was a small whimper, such as a puppy might give. The bolt came out whole, much to my relief. He had been hit with a dart released from a fairy bow during the hunting of the Host and such shot is deadly. The head is of stone, finely worked and razor sharp. If it snaps off inside the flesh it contains magic enough to work its way through the veins to the heart. I cleaned the wound as best I could, using my kerchief and brandy from my flask, and then doffed my hat, wishing him goodnight. I had done what I could for him and animals have ways to cure themselves.

'We have been friends ever since.' Jack Cade leaned over to pat the shaggy head. 'He has come to my aid more than once. Let us pray that he will do the same again. Now hold tight.'

He ducked his head under dripping branches. They were coming down off the high heathland, entering a patch of scrubby wood. Once through that, Jack spurred his horse to a canter and the Guytrash increased his easy lope. A muffled clang, as of metal on stone, pierced the silence and both animals increased their pace. They were sure footed, although the mist had now thickened to such a degree that visibility was almost down to nil on the broad trackway that led towards Dwerry Hollow.

The fog was like wet cotton wool as Jack and Davey entered the Hollow, and it was very chill, like riding into a deep freeze. Dell's hooves made no sound; padding over the tarmac as if bound with cloth.

Jack dismounted and lifted Davey down. The Guytrash yawned and lay on the ground, head on his paws, like a gigantic labrador. The highwayman put his finger to his lips in warning to make no sound as they stole up to the rear of the building. Access would be no problem for him, he could glide through solid doors and walls. Davey, however, was a different matter. He would have to find a more conventional way in.

He nearly fell through the trap door left open by the others. It was suddenly there before him, a wide black space. He stumbled, muttering swear words, and then stopped to listen, hoping that his stifled exclamation had not alerted whoever lay inside.

Jack Cade slowly eased his sword from its scabbard and motioned to go forward. Together they stole down the basement steps; pausing every few paces to make sure their presence remained undetected. It was vital to keep the element of surprise.

14

'Tom doesn't know anything!' Kate was pleading. 'Let him go!'

The Lady held the girl with her eyes. The colour seemed to shift from silver to black and back again, like moonlight on oil.

'She's telling the truth,' she said at last, gesturing for the clown to release Tom from his hold.

The clown gave the boy's hair one last pull and his arm one last vicious twist before sending him skidding on his knees across the room.

'What do you want with us?'

'My business is not with you, as such,' the Lady sneered.

Her mood was curdling. The rest of the paltry ghost crew she had recruited had come back empty-handed. They were skulking in the corner now, trying to avoid her anger. As well they might. Their failure meant that the one she really wanted was still free and she was encumbered with these others. She surveyed the two girls and the boy the Clown had been mauling. They were almost full-grown, far too old for her purposes. They were superfluous and she would make them suffer for it.

'You are a mere irritation,' she went on. 'My business is

223

with this child here – and your brother. He robbed me, cheated me. We do not take such insults lightly. An eye for an eye, was ever our way.' Her hand tightened on Emma's shoulder. 'He must pay the price.'

'Not Emma. Please!' Kate was desperate.

'Oh?' The Lady's laughter was full of hatred and contempt. 'Then whom do you suggest?'

'What are you going to do to her? Please don't hurt her . . .'

'Who said anything about hurting her?' The grip on the child's shoulder softened. 'No one will hurt her. I just want to keep her. We will have a lovely time together.' Long fingers stroked Emma's pale cheek. 'Won't we, my pet?'

'What about Davey?' Kate asked faintly. 'Do you want to keep him, too?'

'Keep him?' The Lady frowned. 'Oh, no. I don't want to keep him. I just want to punish him,' she said simply, her red mouth stretching in a smile as her eyes filmed to black.

'Well I'm here. So you can let them go.'

Kate turned, her eyes widening, as Davey stepped into the room.

'No, Davey!' She shook her head frantically. 'She means you harm! You have to get away from here!'

Davey had gone for maximum surprise and got it. They were all staring at him in varying degrees of astonishment. It was important to keep it that way, make them focus on him alone. Even though Davey knew that Jack was right behind him, he hesitated for a moment, almost faltering. His knees seemed to turn to water and the fear he felt threatened to overwhelm him. His little sister was in the grip of the Old Grey Man's daughter and to her right he caught sight of that loathsome ghost crew skulking in the shadows.

'It – it's all right, Kate,' he said, trying to keep his voice from shaking. 'This is between her and me. There's no need for you to be involved.' He looked at the woman. 'It's because of that kid, isn't it? The one I stopped you from taking?'

The Lady inclined her head.

'Well, I – I'm glad I did it,' the words came out in a rush. 'And – and I'm prepared to pay the price for it, but there is one thing . . .'

'And what is that?' She smiled down at him, as though amused, intrigued by his audacity.

'I'm, I'm,' Davey paused, trying to keep his voice level, aware of the need to play for time, to gain her attention and keep it. To do that, he must appear calm on the outside, even though every time he looked at her his insides shrivelled with fear. 'I'm prepared to go with you, but you must let the others go.' He nodded towards his little sister. 'That means Emma, too.'

'I see,' her smile grew wider and she glanced towards the ghost crew, who drew nearer, eager to join in the joke.

'Those are my terms.' Davey threw his head back, squaring his shoulders, hoping he looked much braver than he felt. 'Take 'em, or leave 'em.'

She held her head on one side, as though considering his words. Then her mood changed. Her attention was fully on Davey now. She narrowed her slanting eyes and he felt her silver gaze searing deep down inside. When she spoke her voice was clear and cold with the clashing ring of a glass bell.

'And what makes you think,' she pointed towards him with a long pale finger, the nail filed to a point like sheathed silver. 'What makes you think that *you* can parlay with *me*?'

The ghost crew were gathering under the sloping window, their greedy eyes on Davey and the other children. The boy was no match for the Lady and she only had use for the smallest, she had promised the others to them. They shuffled forward sensing that this confrontation would shortly be coming to a close.

'What gives you the right, Davey Williams? Oh, you will be punished for this impertinence. I will—'

'Will you, Lady?' Jack Cade spoke from the shadows, Davey's performance had allowed him time to sneak in unnoticed. 'I do not think so.' He drew his sword. 'Let these children go.'

'Who speaks here?' Her voice hissed like steel on ice. 'Who seeks to interfere?'

'Jack Cade, at your service.' The highwayman stepped

226

forward and gave a sweeping mock bow. 'Now unhand
the child.'

'This is not your quarrel, Jack Cade. If you go now, no
harm will come to you.'

'These children are under my protection. Their quarrel
is my quarrel. I owe them a debt of blood.'

He strode closer but the Lady showed no sign of
backing away, or releasing Emma. The ghost crew were
stirring restlessly, uncertain as to what to do. They formed
themselves into a semicircle and began advancing on him.
The two smaller figures, one black, one white, either side
of the clown. Jack swept his sword in a blurring arc,
warning them off, making them cringe back, before
bringing it round to the front again. He held the hilt
with two hands pointing the sword towards the Lady.

'Do not seek to threaten me with that toy, highwayman,' she laughed at him, throwing her head back in
sneering contempt. 'Do you not know who I am?'

'I know well enough, Lady.'

'Then you know that I am Queen of this place.
Nothing can harm me here. Dwerry Hollow belonged
to me and my kind long before men came to grub in the
ground for stone to build their pathetic hovels, and we
will be here long after they have gone. You cannot harm
me with your weapons . . .'

'I know you do not fear the blade, Lady,' Jack Cade
said, bringing the sword up in front of her face. 'But I have
heard that your kind like not the metal.' As he moved the

hilt, the naked steel took on a dull, blue shine. 'Is that not so?'

She locked him with her gaze, her grip on Emma tightened and her eyes blazed defiance. Kate held her breath, as the two adults stared at each other. The confrontation was in such fine balance that she had no idea which way it would go.

Next to her Davey bit his lip, almost hard enough to draw blood. If the Lady won, he dared not think what would happen. Jack was their last hope — almost. The moment seemed to stretch forever, Jack's sword getting closer and closer, then the Lady flinched back.

'I have heard that the touch of iron is such that you feel it like a branding,' he said, low and menacing. 'Shall we put it to the test?' He thrust the sword closer until the flat of the blade was almost touching her pale skin. She jerked her head away, her nostrils flaring as if at something repellent. 'I see not. Let the child go.'

The children watched, hardly daring to breathe. Then, to their intense relief, one by one the long silver-tipped fingers released their hold on Emma's shoulder.

'You cannot get away, Jack Cade. You are outnumbered,' she hissed, looking round desperately for her ghost crew. 'On him!' she screamed at them. 'He is only one! Seize him! What is the matter with you? Are you afraid of a lone man and a gaggle of children? You cowardly—'

As much as they feared her anger, their attention was directed away from her. There was something above them, prowling up and down outside the long sloping window, casting a massive shadow.

Judging the moment to be right, Jack gave a piercing whistle. He seized the child from the Lady's slackened grip and leapt back across the room, throwing himself in front of Davey and the other children, seeking to shelter them with his body.

Glass showered in all directions as the Guytrash crashed through the window. The huge creature sprang down with his red eyes blazing and front legs extended. His huge mouth yawned wide to show ranks of long white teeth. The ghost crew left it a fraction too late to get out of the way. They stared up in frozen panic; hands raised in a futile effort to fend him off.

The children clutched on to Jack for protection, cowering away from the hideous shrieks and screams as the huge creature landed with a blood chilling snarl right on top of the ghost crew. The Guytrash tore into them with long curving claws, pulling them apart with teeth as long and sharp as daggers. Gradually the cries died down and all that was left for him to worry at was a heap of bones, and a bundle of shredded rags: white, red and black.

'So, Jack Cade, this time you win.'

The Lady spoke, her voice and form growing thin. At the sound of her, the Guytrash looked up and began to growl deep in his throat. His back leg twitched, as if at the memory of an old injury. High on the hip, one white streak of fur snaked in and out of the black. She stepped back and away as the huge creature lumbered to his feet.

'Be warned, Davey Williams,' she turned on him, her lovely face twisted with loathing even as it faded, one arm extended towards him, the fingers held out in a stiff fingered gesture of cursing. 'Be warned by me! There is more than one way to fell a tree!'

And then she was gone. The Guytrash was left growling at thin air. He gave a whine of frustration and turned to go back through the window. He looked once behind him, his huge eyes shining like traffic lights. Jack took his hat off and bowed, wishing him goodnight. The huge dog wagged his great tail and bounded away, taking a height of six metres in one great stretching leap and disappeared back into the night.

'What did she mean?' Davey asked, his voice shaking. 'That thing she said about the tree?'

The Lady's hostility had deeply upset him. Her venomous hatred had frightened him far more than anything else that had happened that night. He had never seen or felt such fury before, especially not directed at him. It was still misty outside, although the fog was lifting. Reluctantly, Davey moved from the shelter of the building and looked around cautiously, fearful that she might still be lurking about somewhere, waiting to pounce on him like an angry wild cat.

'Who is to say?' Jack replied with a shrug. The strength

230

of her malediction had disturbed him, too. He was seeking to give comfort he did not feel. 'They ever speak in riddles. It is their way. Do not concern yourself with her. You must look to your sister.' He pointed to Emma who was standing with Kate's coat wrapped round her. 'Where is your father, your mother? Are they at home?'

'No. They've gone to a party. That's how all this started.'

'Where is this party?'

'Out near Kingswood, I'm not sure exactly – that was part of the trouble . . .'

'Will they be long away?'

'I don't know,' Davey shook his head. 'They aren't usually very late, but what with this fog . . .' He paused to think. 'It'll be all right on the bypass, but once they come on to the road by the river – it's usually bad down there.'

'The Old Forest Road?'

'Yes. But why?' Davey looked up at the highwayman, puzzled by his interest.

'Never mind. As I said, your job now is to get your sister home and keep her safe. Make all speed.' He was speaking to all of them now. 'And once in, lock your doors and windows and stay together. Do not answer to anyone unless you are very sure of the caller. Anybody at all, do you hear me?'

'What if we know them?' Tom asked.

'Tell me, Thomas,' Jack put his arm across the boy's shoulder. 'The Lady, the Old Grey Man's daughter – what does she look like?'

Tom looked at him, surprised. They had only seen her a minute ago, so it seemed a pretty silly question to ask, but he knew Jack to be anything but stupid.

'We-ell,' he began. 'She's got this dead white skin and a bright red mouth and pale eyes and hair, and—'

'No,' Kate interrupted. 'That's not right. She's got jet-black hair and black eyes, and high cheek bones, and—'

'No,' Davey shook his head. 'You are both wrong. She has silvery hair and eyes like mercury . . .'

'There, do you see?' Jack Cade looked round at them. 'You all looked together and saw different things. She can take any shape she pleases. You cannot trust your eyes only. She can make you see what you have in your mind. She can even take the shape of your own mother, so as I say,' he mounted his horse, 'take care whom you let in your house. Now, farewell. I must away.'

'Aren't you coming with us?' Davey looked up at him.

'I will see you safe to your door, but then I have other work to do.'

'Like what?'

'You need not concern yourself.'

'Jack, wait! When will we see you again?'

Davey hung on to his stirrup and trotted along beside him, but there was no way to prevent him from leaving. The highwayman was already fading . . .

'I will come when there is need, just like tonight.' Jack's voice came from the air above him. 'Now off home with you. I'll be watching, even if you cannot see me.'

He shadowed them back to their house, and then turned and spurred his horse up on to the Heath. He went in search of the Old Grey Man's daughter. He did not want to alarm the children, but he did not think that her meddling was finished. She was devious and cunning and her business here was far from over. If she could not attack the children directly, she would find another way.

Jack broke into a gallop, directing Dell towards the road which wound through the tract of ancient woodland that lay to the west of Wesson Heath. It was still Hallowe'en and the Old Forest Road lay within her domain. He would not rest until the night was out.

15

Kate and Elinor took Emma upstairs while Davey prepared a hot water bottle for her bed. They washed her hands and face as best they could and changed her into fresh pyjamas. The yellow ones she had on were all dusty and cobwebby. They looked her over carefully. On the outside, she seemed all right. She was not cold. Her colour was good. She was breathing normally. She obeyed instructions and could walk around after a fashion, which was a good thing, or they would never have got her home, but all the time her eyes were closed. It was as if she was sleepwalking or in some kind of trance.

'Maybe she'll snap out of it,' Elinor said as they bundled her into bed.

'I hope so,' Kate frowned. 'Goodness knows what we'll tell Mum and Dad if she doesn't.'

Emma gave a little grunt and rolled herself up into a tight ball. She stuck her thumb in her mouth and burrowed down under the duvet.

'She hasn't sucked her thumb for years,' Kate said as she slipped the hot water bottle in at her feet and turned the top edge of the duvet back. 'I think we ought to sleep in here.' She turned to Elinor. 'That way we can keep an eye on her.'

Elinor nodded. 'I'll get my gear.'

'What about the boys?' she asked as she came back, arms full of sleeping bags and bedding.

Kate wrinkled her nose. 'I don't think we want them in here, too. It's only a very small room and have you smelt Davey's feet with his trainers off?'

Ellie giggled, 'Er, yes. Tom's just as bad. I hadn't thought of that.'

'Anyway,' Kate went on, 'Emma wouldn't like it. She's strictly into girl power, look at the posters she's got in here. She's very fussy about who comes in and boys are not invited.'

'That's all right,' Davey's voice came from outside the door. 'We just came up to see if you're OK, but we know when we're not wanted. Don't we, Tom?'

'We certainly do.'

'Do you fancy something to eat?'

'Yes, I'm starving.'

'Me, too. Let's see what there is in the fridge. I think there's some pizza left.'

'Sounds like a good idea.'

Now that they were back in the house, safe and sound, Tom and Davey both found that they were very hungry.

'What are you doing in here?'

Kate looked up, squinting in the glow from the Owl and the Pussycat nightlight, to see Emma's blue eyes staring at her over the edge of the bed. Next to her on the floor Ellie stirred and turned over, burying her head down into her sleeping bag.

'Shh,' Kate put a finger to her lips. 'We don't want to wake Ellie. We just thought you might be scared, that's all. We thought you might like company.'

'That's not what you said earlier,' Emma replied in a fierce whisper, remembering the rough ride Kate had given her at bedtime. 'You said—'

'Yes, well, we changed our minds.' Kate struggled up into a sitting position. 'Anyway, are you OK? How do you feel?'

'All right,' Emma replied. 'Why shouldn't I be?' She gave an enormous yawn and looked down at herself. 'Why am I in these?' she said, pulling at the front of her pink pyjamas. 'I'm sure I had the yellow ones on . . .' Her face began to pucker with uncertainty.

'You, you had a bad dream,' Kate said quickly. 'You were shouting out and you'd got all hot and sweaty, so I changed you into those. Then Ellie and I moved our stuff in, just in case it happened again.'

'Oh, right.'

To Kate's relief, Emma seemed to swallow the explanation.

'Try and go back to sleep now,' she said as her little sister lay back down.

'I remember my dream now,' Emma said after a while. 'And it *was* very scary. There was this horrible clown . . .' She shivered a little at the memory. 'He put me on his back and took me out of the house. He came and got me even though you were all downstairs, talking and laughing with the TV on and everything, because I was all by myself . . . Anyway, then I was in this big old house – it was horrible, all cold and creepy and full of cobwebs and there was this woman. I though it was Mum at first, that was the worst thing. She looked like Cruella DeThingummy . . .'

'Cruella DeVille,' Kate supplied.

'That's right!' Emma shuddered. 'I don't like her. I didn't want Mum to dress up as her, but I thought she'd be cross if I said so . . .'

'This woman, the one in the dream, I mean. Did she,' Kate hesitated, wondering how to put this. 'Did she do anything to you?'

'No,' Emma shook her head slowly. 'She was just creepy. Like she was trying to be nice, but underneath I could tell she was really nasty. She had horrid cold hands.' Emma shivered again. 'And this voice that crackled like ice. There were others with the clown, dressed up like for trickle treat, they were nasty, too, and they were all scared of her, she was the boss, I could tell. It was strange . . .' Emma broke off for a moment. 'Then you were there, you and Ellie and Tom and then Davey – with a highwayman – weird – and then,' she laughed softly to herself, 'this huge giant dog came jumping through the window and ate the clown up – and his horrible mates. The Cruella woman disappeared and everything was all right after that. Dreams are funny, don't you think?' She twisted round in bed to look down at her sister. 'Do you have dreams like that?'

'Yes.' Kate hugged her knees through the sleeping bag. 'Sometimes. You go back to sleep now.'

Within a few minutes, regular breathing showed Emma to be sleeping soundly. Elinor had stopped wriggling her protest at being disturbed and was stretched out on her back snoring ever so slightly. Kate pulled her own sleeping bag up to her chin and lay waiting for sleep to come. She was really tired, but couldn't sleep now. Every time she closed her eyes, images from the past night came flashing into her mind: the Lady's mocking smile, the clown's painted grin, the eyes of the Guytrash. Her relief at Emma being all right and thinking it all a dream was rapidly turning into anxiety. Worries wove her thoughts into webs of fear: what if she was still out there? What if she came after them? There was still no sign of Mum and Dad. How could ordinary locks and bolts keep her out? Kate turned over, burying her head in the pillow, telling herself that she was being silly, getting as bad as Emma. Everything was going to be fine. Nothing else could happen now, surely?

16

'I can't see a thing.' Stephen Williams leaned forward to wipe at the windscreen again.

'There's no point in doing that,' his wife replied from the driving seat. 'It's on the outside, not in.'

She peered into the gloom in front of her. The fog was getting worse, if anything.

'Put the full beam on,' her husband suggested.

She shook her head. Full beam flared off the dense bank, turning it into a solid wall of whiteness.

'It'll take forever, at this rate.' He shifted in his seat and folded his arms.

'It'll take as long as it takes,' his wife replied without looking at him. 'There's no point in getting impatient.'

'We should have found another route. The fog's always bad down here.'

He looked out of the window. The Old Forest Road was narrow and the trees grew in close; their twisted branches loomed out of the fog like clutching arms.

'It's bad everywhere and this is the most direct road. All the others involve a big detour.'

'We *could* turn back.'

'But we're more than halfway home!' She took her eyes

off the road and turned to him. 'What would be the point?'

'Alison! Watch out!'

He jammed his foot down on an imaginary brake pedal, but his wife had already depressed the real one. There was a horseman riding right in front of them. Where on earth had he come from? If she had not been going so slowly she would have hit him.

By her side, her husband groaned, 'That's *all* we need! I don't *believe* it! That takes the biscuit!'

'Stephen, will you stop moaning! You are not helping!'

He leaned over to sound the horn.

'Don't do that,' his wife pushed his hand away. 'You'll startle the horse.'

'So what? He's taking up half the road. The chap must be drunk. Coming back from a fancy dress party judging by the way he's dressed. Can you be drunk in charge of a horse?'

'I suppose so. I don't know.'

The fog thinned briefly, allowing her to see that the rider in front of her was dressed like a highwayman. He looked rather romantic, in his cocked hat and velvet coat, with wisps of mist swirling around him. But Alison was in no mood for romantic images, she just wanted to get home as quickly as possible and he was holding her up. She pulled out on to the other side of the road. The way ahead was clear, but the rider seemed to anticipate and shadow her movements and she still could not get past him. He slowed again to walking pace. It was almost as if he was playing a game.

By her side, her husband groaned. 'He's doing that on purpose! The fog seems to be lifting a bit and this is the only straight piece of road for miles. If it wasn't for him, you could really put your foot down. Go on, Ali, get past him!'

She steered the car out and back again. 'I can't. There's just not enough room.'

Her husband snorted contempt. 'If *I* was driving . . .'

'But you're not, are you? Because you've had too much to drink. So why don't you be quiet and let me get on with it.'

'We could be here all night . . .'

'I'm sure he'll move over when the verge widens.'

Stephen had a point, she thought, they were really crawling. The road stretched away straight, for about half a mile, before curving into the first of a series of bends. They passed the warning sign at walking pace. Stephen had gone to sleep, or was pretending, and at least there was no build-up of cars behind, with impatient drivers all scowling at her. In fact, they hadn't seen any other traffic, which was odd.

Alison peered at the road ahead. This was known to be a dangerous bend. It began as a gentle curve and it was easy to misjudge, especially when travelling at speed. Not a problem tonight, of course, what with the horse . . .

What was happening now? The rider had stopped altogether. Alison jammed on the brakes, jerking the car and waking Stephen.

'What's up? What's the matter?'

'I don't know. He's just stopped in the middle of the road.'

'I told you we should have sorted him out. You are just hopeless, Alison. You didn't make enough of an effort to get past him. I'll deal with this.' Stephen wound the window down. 'Hey, mate!' he yelled. 'Get out of the way!'

In front of them, the highwayman's horse reared and turned. The rider wore a mask over his eyes; he looked down at the car and smiled. Long dark curling hair streamed on to his shoulders as he removed his hat and waved it as if in farewell. He turned back in the saddle and kicked his heel into his horse's flank. She wheeled, as obedient and elegant as a circus mount, before leaping off and away.

Alison and Stephen blinked at the windscreen and stared.

'Did you see that?' he asked.

She nodded. Neither wanted to say it out loud, but horse and rider seemed to leave the road and jump into nowhere. In the time it took to wink an eye they seemed to completely disappear.

Instead . . . Instead . . .

Stephen took a quick intake of breath. A huge old

forest oak had fallen right across the road, sprawling over to the other side. Thick shards of white heart wood stuck up, torn and splintered, where the trunk had sheered off from its base in the verge. The great tree was metres across; its branches were sticking up to the sky, spreading out on either side. It was as if an impenetrable thicket had suddenly sprung up in the middle of the road.

'My God!'

Alison paled, putting her hand to her mouth. Because of the curve in the road, the fallen tree was invisible from even a few metres away. If they had been travelling at any speed, any speed at all, they would have ploughed right into it. If it had not been for that horseman, they would have been killed. She wound her window down and looked out. There was absolutely no sign of him. She listened but the woods were silent. There was no sound of hoof beats. They were completely alone.

Alison had to sit still for a moment or two to compose herself. Stephen sat by her side, entirely sober now.

'Are you OK to drive?' he asked her.

She nodded, turning her head to gauge the road behind her, but her hands were still shaking when she put the car into reverse and she could hardly keep her foot steady on the clutch pedal. She backed the car up and turned it round while Stephen put out the warning triangles that they carried in the car. Their priority was to get to a

17

They were sleeping with the bedroom door open. The clash of keys being dropped into the bowl in the hall woke Kate.

'I thought we were *never* going to get home,' she heard her mother say.

Kate struggled out of her sleeping bag and crept down the stairs. 'Hi, Mum.'

'Hi, Katie. How's it been?'

'Oh, OK.' Kate replied warily.

'Emma been all right?' her mum asked.

Kate nodded. 'Zoe didn't show up, though.'

'I know. There was some kind of mix-up. Sorry about that. Did you cope?'

'Yes. We coped fine.'

'Good. All safe and sound now, eh?'

'Yes.' Kate nodded again. 'But I was expecting you back ages ago. What took you so long?'

'Don't ask.' Both her parents looked pale and tired, a look exaggerated by their fancy dress clothes and make up.

'We've had a hell of a journey back,' her father said.

'Why?' Kate asked. 'What happened?'

'Never mind.' He shook his head and smiled. 'You wouldn't believe me if I told you.'

Up in his room, Davey was relieved to hear his parents come in. He had been lying awake worrying, his mind filled with terrible anxiety. He feared the Old Grey Man's daughter and what she might do. Davey had thwarted her twice. He knew her to be capable of anything and without Jack's protection, he felt weak and vulnerable. Even if she did not attack him directly, she would find a way to get back at him through Mum, Dad, his family; but everyone was safe home now, under one roof together. He turned over, pulling the duvet up round his ears, waiting for sleep to claim him.

It could have been the wail of a siren that woke him, jerking him into consciousness. The familiar call an ambulance or fire engine made as it screamed through the village, speeding to some emergency. The sound came, waxing and waning as if on the wind, and seemed to go on for a long time. Davey lay in bed, shivering and terrified. The noise seemed to pierce right into him, spreading dread and fear through his mind. It could have been a siren, he told himself, it could have been . . .

Something inside him, some deep intuition, told him that this was not so. He had heard the call of the *bean sidhe*, the *banshee*. It was the ancient cry of the fairy woman, howling out her frustration, screaming a wordless warning, telling him that this was not over, it was far from over. Hallowe'en might have passed, but what had begun at midsummer was set to continue . . .

A TRAP IN TIME

Celia Rees

Part two of the chilling trilogy that began with *City of Shadows*

All through the city and its suburbs, the past lies behind the present and ghosts shadow the living. There are threshold zones, borderlines, and places where the laws of time and space falter. Strange things can happen, the barriers between the worlds grow thin and it is possible, just possible, to move from world to another . . .

Davey had hoped that the chilling events of Midsummer and Halloween were all part of a terrible dream – a dream he never wants to have again. But Christmas brings a new horror: Davey's archenemy, the Lady, is back to get revenge . . . and an archaeological dig uncovers more than just an old building. For Davey, Elinor, Kate and Tom, it unleashes a terrifying and unearthly force, which they will need all their strength, and Davey's gift for Second Sight, to resist . . .

THE HOST RIDES OUT

Celia Rees

The final part in a compelling trilogy

All through the city and its suburbs, the past lies behind the present and ghosts shadow the living. There are threshold zones, borderlines, and places where the laws of time and space falter. Strange things can happen, the barriers between the worlds grow thin and it is possible, just possible, to move from world to another . . .

Paranormal activity is causing chaos for all who live and work in the city. And Davey is more alert than his sister and cousins to voices from the past. Will the ghosthunter – brought in to investigate – uncover the root of the problem, or is his very presence a trigger for evil spirits to make themselves known . . ? And now Davey must be more on his guard than ever. When Midsummer comes round again, his icily dangerous nemesis, the Lady, will stop at nothing to banish him to a life in hell . . .